WICKED SONG

A WICKEDLY SPICY FAIRYTALE RETELLING

WICKED EVERMORE
BOOK TWO

INES JOHNSON

FORBIDDEN FOREST
THORNHALL
GREYM
SNOW KINGDOMS
FENVALEN
VALEBRI
RAVENHOLD
COASTAL KINGDOMS
TIDEHAVEN
INL
SEA KINGDOMS
E

EVERMORE

CURSED REALMS
BEAST LANDS
GDOMS
OREST
FIRE ISLANDS

PROLOGUE

Not so long ago, in the deep blue sea...

THE WATER SHIMMERED like liquid obsidian near a tangle of coral. Bioluminescent fish flickered around the plant life, their pale glow casting eerie, shifting shadows against the reef. The sea was calm, a deceptive lull that stretched in every direction. Its gentle undulations betrayed none of the conflict simmering beneath its surface.

Ursula's hand brushed against something slick and foreign. She recoiled instinctively, her lip curling in disgust as a half-submerged human bottle bobbed past her fingers, its label peeled and curling from salt and time. A cloud of murky residue trailed from its broken neck, polluting the water with its filth. She exhaled sharply, baring her teeth.

Humans treated the sea like their personal waste bin, discarding their refuse as if the tides existed to swallow their sins. She flicked her wrist, sending the bottle spiraling away, but her annoyance remained. It clung to her like a second skin. Ahead of her, a bright shape flitted through the current, darting between drifting debris.

"Ariel," she called out, "stay away from that ship."

But like any guppy who thought they knew every current, Ariel ignored her aunt's warning and swam ahead, undaunted.

Ursula clenched her jaw, trying to ignore the simmering resentment that had become as much a part of her as the pulse of the tides. Ariel had never been told 'no' in her life, and it showed in the way she ignored warnings like they were merely inconvenient suggestions.

It was something Ursula couldn't get away with. Her father had forbidden her from attending the upcoming diplomatic summit, claiming it was a meeting for kings and commanders—not daughters with "strong opinions." Ursula hadn't pouted or wept. She'd done what any cunning strategist would: gone around her father's trident and whispered her ideas directly to her older brother.

She'd told Triton that the real solution to the mounting tension between the sea and the surface didn't lie with the Inland King—whose claims over the Enchanted Forest were mostly ceremonial, given that the Forest Guardian and the faefolk ruled the roots and wilds. Nor was the Frost Queen of the northern mountains the true obstacle, despite her glacial disdain for coastal expansion. The crux of the issue, Ursula had explained, lay with the Coastal Kingdom—their docks, their refuse, their overfishing. If they wanted peace, Triton had to secure an alliance with the Coast King, whose subjects were the ones dumping nets and poisons into their waters.

Ursula had even devised a clever trade system—ocean routes in exchange for coastal protection spells to ward off sea monsters and access to rare herbs in the sea's depths in exchange for proper waste filtering at the border harbors. It was a plan that could have changed everything.

And what had her brilliant older brother done?

He'd swum right into the meeting chamber with a proud flick of his tail and presented her ideas as if they'd emerged from the coral crown of his own head. From what she'd heard from her spies, their father had clapped his son on the back, praising Triton's initiative, while Ursula's seat at the table remained empty. Worse still, her whale of a brother had attached his little barnacle to Ursula, placing Ariel as Ursula's responsibility for the duration of the talks.

If only Ursula had treated that request like the inconvenient suggestion it was instead of obeying like some dutiful, exiled aunt.

Ursula kicked harder, propelling herself forward. The pressure of the water squeezed against her ribs as she narrowed the distance between her and the princess. A burst of bubbles reached her ears before the sight of red hair did. If an onlooker didn't know any better, they would say Ursula and Ariel were twins. They favored each other not only in hair color and skin tones but also in the eyes. The difference was that Ursula had the curves that came with one approaching womanhood, while Ariel still had the gangly fins of a guppy.

The girl twirled in delight, her grabby hands clutching a tiny trident of tarnished silver. She opened her mouth, and more bubbles burst forth, carrying a high-pitched sound. It was a language woven from notes that could vibrate through the bones of anything that swam near. Had Ursula walked on two legs instead of fins, the sound of her niece's voice could compel her to do anything the siren wanted. But a siren's call didn't work on another siren, or on that siren's true love.

Ariel had been born a true siren. She had no voice box to shape words or twist around syllables. Instead, she produced sound the way whales and dolphins did—sonar pulses that rippled through the water in piercing, melodic waves. A school of fish nearby flinched at the sound and veered away, sensing a presence more powerful than themselves. Predators lurking in the dark would also recognize the unmistakable pitch of a siren and keep their distance.

Look at this stuff! Ariel sang, holding out the human object. *Isn't it neat?*

Ursula scoffed, crossing her arms. She didn't need to send a note back—her silence was answer enough. Ariel, ever stubborn, let out another rippling pulse, this one insistent, prodding.

You're such a jellyfish, Aunt Ursula.

Her? A jellyfish? Ursula let out a low, almost imperceptible hum. The kind of barely there response that wasn't words but a feeling: annoyance.

I can take care of myself. You don't have to fin-sit me.

No sooner did the last note pass the princess' lips than a hulking, vast shadow drifted above them. A beast of wood and iron, its underbelly riddled with barnacles and ghostly strands of seaweed. The scent of oil and something acrid, something wrong, stained the water around it.

Ariel's wide blue eyes reflected the flickering light from the ship's lanterns.

Ursula knew that look. It was the same look her walrus of a big brother got when he was about to do something reckless that he'd find a way to blame her for.

"Ariel, don't you dare."

Ariel couldn't form words, but she understood them just fine. Except when she wanted to ignore them, to chase after her own interests. Ariel's response was a mischievous burst of high-pitched clicks, the under-water equivalent of a giggle. She turned and darted toward the surface.

Ursula cursed, loosing a sharp, urgent note—one meant to stop prey in its tracks. Except Ariel wasn't prey. The sea princess was at the top of the food chain under the sea. So while Ursula's note rolled out like a shockwave, commanding, undeniable, something that would have made any lesser creature freeze in place, Ariel ignored it.

With a quick flick of her tail, Ariel shot forward, closer to the ship, closer to the danger.

Ursula pushed off the reef in pursuit. The water swirled around her in a cyclone of frustration. Her powerful strokes carved through the deep. She surged forward, grabbing Ariel's wrist and yanking her back with more force than necessary.

The younger girl yelped.

"You reckless little guppy. Do you have any idea what humans do to creatures like us?"

Ariel wrenched her arm free, stubbornness flashing across her delicate features. *Can you imagine all the treasures up there?*

"They have no treasures. They trade in junk, and they'll throw you in a net. Or worse."

They're not all bad. Ariel jutted her chin toward the ship. *Not everyone is trying to hurt us.*

A splash overhead. A human voice, sharp and guttural. Then came the thunk of something heavy piercing the water.

A harpoon. It missed them by mere inches, sinking into the seabed below.

"Not all bad?" Ursula seethed, shoving Ariel behind her. "Tell me again, little princess—what part of that looks like it isn't trying to hurt you?"

A second harpoon cut through the water, closer this time. Ursula shoved Ariel downward, dragging her away from the ship's shadow.

"Swim," she ordered. "Now."

For once, Ariel obeyed.

A third harpoon sliced through the water, its deadly tip a silver blur against the dark. It grazed

Ursula's arm as it shot past. A burning sting sliced across her skin.

A sharp *thwip* cut through the current. Then a sickening thunk. Ariel's body jerked. Her song cut off in a choked, soundless scream. The harpoon had struck just below her ribs. Its wicked barbs snagged against soft flesh, and the force of the impact spun the child in the water like a broken doll.

Ursula lunged, catching Ariel before she could drift. Warm blood—too warm, too much—spilled into the sea, curling around them in ghostly tendrils.

Another harpoon shot past. Rage swallowed fear whole. Ursula opened her mouth and sang.

Her siren's song was not high-pitched and happy like her niece's. Ursula's dark song tore through the ocean in deep, resonant waves, slicing through the water like a shockwave, a command, a summons, a reckoning.

Miles away, deep within a trench untouched by light, a massive eye blinked open, and the sea shuddered. The shift in the current could be felt on the sea's floor, through the floorboards of the hulking ship. Shadows raced across the surface of the waters. Waves rolled outward as something enormous rose from the depths.

The ship's hull groaned. The sound was loud enough to pierce the veil of the waters. Then the shouting began. It was no use. Even though it was miles away, there was no way the sailors would outrun what lurked in the deep.

The kraken breached the surface. A monstrous limb, thick as a hundred ship masts, broke the surface in an explosion of white water. The sky darkened beneath its shadow. The humans screamed.

A single colossal tentacle slammed down upon the ship. The impact sent a crack through the air, louder than thunder, as the mast splintered like dry driftwood. The vessel tilted wildly, men and cargo spilling into the sea in a chaotic, flailing mass. Then the real carnage began.

The moment their fragile bodies touched the water, the ocean came alive.

Sharks.

Serpents.

Predators that lurked in the depths, drawn by the scent of human blood and panic. The humans did not stand a chance. Spoils of their trade—chests, barrels, metal, and glass—sank into the abyss, swallowed whole by the tides.

The ocean turned red. The seabed became a toxic graveyard as bodies and trinkets sank. Ursula didn't spare the scene a glance, but Ariel did.

Trembling in her arms, the sea princess twisted just enough to look back. The pain left her eyes, and wonder took its place. Not wonder at the carnage above her but curiosity at the items falling to pollute the seabed.

Ursula wanted to shake her, but she couldn't. It would probably damage the girl even more. But not as much damage as she'd just done calling the kraken to aid her against the humans. She'd saved Ariel, but she highly doubted her father or brother would ever save her a seat at the table for her troubles.

CHAPTER ONE

P resent Day

THE STEADY SCRATCH of a quill against parchment filled the king's office, the only sound beyond the distant crash of waves against the harbor walls. But it wasn't the king who sat behind the desk. The royal rump hadn't been in this office for at least the last five years.

Prince Eric sat behind his father's desk, the heavy mahogany stretching wide before him, its surface polished to a gleam beneath the glow of candlelight. The scent of ink, old paper, and briny sea air seeped through the cracks of the tall windows, mixing with the tension tightening his chest. The wood chair beneath him was carved and aged, refusing even the smallest comfort. His father had once sat here on a pile of plush cushions. Eric had done away with them the day he first assumed his place at the desk, choosing instead to feel the raw edge of power against his spine. The weight of the crown didn't need softening. This was a hard job. It should feel hard.

His fingers curled around the edge of the latest financial ledger, his thumb brushing over the embossed royal crest. Fewer shipwrecks this year. Fewer men lost. The numbers reflected it—the kingdom's trade had stabilized, thanks to his efforts.

Thanks, he thought begrudgingly, to King Triton and the trade deal that his father had struck some five years ago. It was a trade deal that Eric would have to pay for. And the bill was coming due soon.

Eric stared at the small velvet box perched at the edge of his desk. Its presence gnawed at his focus, a quiet sentinel of obligation. He reached for it and flipped the lid open. Inside lay a pearl ring—simple, elegant, and impossibly heavy with meaning. The ring had been his mother's. She'd pressed it into his hand on one of her last lucid days. Her brown fingers had somehow looked pale as they flexed around the box, but her voice remained sharp.

"She'll need this."

Eric didn't doubt that Queen Selina had known

about the deal his father and the Sea King had struck. Some days, Eric suspected his mother had arranged it herself. She'd always been the managing sort, adept at maneuvering people like chess pieces—especially his father. She had curbed his worst indulgences with little more than a lifted brow and a clipped word: his womanizing, his gluttony, the gambling that had once risked half the Coastal fleet. Since her death, the man had fallen apart like a once-great ship left to rot at the dock. It was Eric who'd been left to gather the splinters.

Eric exhaled sharply, dragging a hand through the short crop of curls on his head. The alliance had been a hard-won battle of negotiations after the kraken's unexpected appearance had nearly decimated the talks before they even began. But the agreement was working.

The Inland and Coastal Kingdoms, once tenuous neighbors, had grown closer under the banner of shared threat. Eric's father and the Inland King had sealed their mutual interests with a pact of arms, joining forces against the troll invasion festering at the mountain borders.

The Frost Kingdom, ever aloof in its icy perch, had remained neutral—neither pledging troops nor threatening to withdraw from the coalition. Their silence came with its own kind of power. Neutrality from the Frost Matriarchs was a kind of consent. It kept the lines of communication open, should they be needed in future disputes.

The Sea King, and later his son, had honored their word, keeping monsters from the depths at bay, ensuring trade ships safe passage through the routes they had agreed upon—so long as seamen stayed within their lanes. And so long as the Coastal Prince kept his part of the bargain with the Sea King's daughter.

Eric shut the ring box and returned his attention to the ledgers. One particular entry caught his attention. He ran his eyes over the shipments expected over the next few days, then circled back to one route that should not exist. A single ship, an ocean liner, scheduled to leave today and return in two days' time. By the size of the ship as well as its departure date, it should not be back so soon.

A mistake? Or something worse? A knock at the door.

"Come in."

The door creaked open, and Grimsby stepped inside. The older man was tall and wiry, all lean efficiency with no wasted movement. The Coastal Kingdom's chamberlain was a man who had trimmed himself down to the essentials, just as he did with everything else in life. His sharp, hawk-like features were carved from discipline, his dark coat perfectly pressed, not a wrinkle or unnecessary embellishment in sight. Unlike the king he served—who draped himself in rich velvets, gilded buttons, and rings that weighed down his fingers—Grimsby was a man of restraint.

Even his voice, when he spoke, was measured, pared down to its most necessary words. "You sent for me, Your Highness?"

He had sent for the chamberlain on another matter, but the one on the desk before him pressed firmer. If anyone had known about this unauthorized shipment's route, it was Grimsby. Eric pushed the ledger across the desk.

Grimsby adjusted his spectacles before peering at the document. A pause. The candlelight flickered, throwing deep lines across the older man's face. "Ah."

Eric's hands flattened against the desk. "Ah?"

Grimsby sighed, shoulders lowering with the weight of something he didn't want to say. "The king approved this shipment personally."

"And you didn't think to tell me?"

"I had no choice, Your *Highness*. It was an order from His *Majesty*, the king."

Eric heard the comparison loud and clear. The words sent cold irritation spiraling through his ribs. It was a reminder of what he had not yet become. What he could not become—not until his marriage was sealed, until the promises made by his parents and the

Sea King were fulfilled, until he was a husband first and a ruler second.

He didn't want to think about that. Not about the arranged marriage looming before him, a union built on duty, not desire. Not about the fact that he had never met Ariel, the mermaid princess who was the cost of his throne.

Instead, he focused on the immediate threat. This ocean liner would be carrying a season's worth of grain in its belly when it returned. It had left with a third of the gold from the kingdom's coffers to trade with Highlanders of the Northern Seas. If that shipment sank on its way out or on its way back, the coastal people would suffer a harsh few seasons. They might not recover. Worse, if Triton saw the taking of this route as a violation of their agreement, it could cost them more than gold. Eric couldn't let that happen.

"If you'd like, I can send a gull to the captain. They can't be so far out yet that a message can't reach them."

"I'll go myself," Eric said, grabbing his coat from the back of the chair.

"Go?"

"To the docks." Eric was already moving. "I'll take a cutter and intercept before it gets out into open waters and takes that route."

Grimsby followed him to the door, quick and composed despite his visible disapproval. "You must be back in time to receive Princess Ariel," he warned. "If the Sea King believes you are indifferent to this union—"

"I know what's at stake."

His father's decisions might still carry the weight of a crown, but Eric would not let them be his kingdom's undoing.

CHAPTER TWO

The coral had once shimmered like a kingdom of light, a kaleidoscope of pinks, oranges, and reds crowned by fan-like towers and spiraling stone. Now the reef was a skeleton. The ruin groaned beneath the gentle current, pockmarked with broken spires and discolored with the leeching gray of pollution. Fishing nets—torn and tangled—hung like limp banners from its once-proud arches, and beer bottles nestled between coral teeth like the offerings of drunken gods.

Ursula reclined on a bed of sea sponge and trailing kelp, her fin coiled beneath her. The spongy surface shifted with the current, cradling her weight as if the sea itself pampered her. Her back rested against the cold, slick curve of a barnacled column, a relic of some forgotten coral citadel. Salt clung to her skin—sharp, grounding—but her expression was distant, bored, as she watched her companions twist lazily through the water.

Flotsam and Jetsam danced through the ribcage of the ruin, long eel bodies lithe and quick. They had slithered over her body while the moonlight did its own dance on the surface of the water. Last night, their movements had been anything but quick and fleeting. They'd brought her to peak after peak as they raided her booty. The eels were pirates in spirit and sin.

"The boys said they caught sight of a liner veering toward the restricted route," Jetsam drawled, his voice a silken rasp. He coiled up near her elbow, teeth flashing as he eyed her bared breast. "One that's too fat to turn in time."

Every once in a while, sailors gambled and sent a ship through the restricted passages. Those waterways were swifter, the currents faster and more direct—a tempting shortcut for those eager to cut days off a voyage and deliver goods ahead of schedule. But speed came at a cost. The faster lanes wound through waters where sea monsters were known to prowl—territories thick with kelp-choked trenches, sleeping leviathans, and ancient things that didn't take kindly to oars.

It was part of the brilliance of Ursula's contribution to the treaty. She had advised that humans take the slower, safer routes—charting a course with naval escorts and sea folk protection—while leaving the treacherous lanes under Sea Kingdom jurisdiction. The Coastal Crown thought they'd been granted safe trade while her people kept leverage. Because the moment a merchant grew too greedy, too rushed, too arrogant—they'd veer off course, and the Sea Kingdom would still have teeth in the game. Except the Sea Kingdom had pulled out the teeth of the one who had set the trap.

"Carrying gold or grain?" Flotsam asked, appearing behind Ursula like a shadow come to life, brushing his teeth against her neck.

Jetsam shrugged as though it didn't matter when the reality was that it did. The ship was likely carrying gold if it was leaving the port. Some vegetation was hard to grow on the coastal lands, and so the kingdom would trade with inlanders from the North and South for things like grain and certain textiles like cottons.

Ursula shuddered at the thought of that scratchy fabric on her skin. She'd tried on something called a sundress once when on land, spun from woven cotton that chafed like nettles. She'd promptly torn the itchy garment off and stood as the tides intended—naked save for her seashell bra.

It had been a new pair of shells that one of her courtiers had brought back from the eastern seas. The polished clam shells had shimmered with hues of violet and moonlit pearl, bound with braided strands of kelp and coral silk that knotted neatly at the back of her neck. The shells weren't identical—nothing in the sea ever truly was—but they'd cupped her like they had been grown for her alone, smooth and strong and meant to be worn by a queen. She hadn't been wearing it the day her father had kicked her out of the kingdom and had left it behind. She wasn't wearing any bra now.

Flotsam or Jetsam reached for her bare skin. Ursula didn't squirm at their renewed attentions, but she didn't lean into it either. She'd already had her fill, and she was done.

She was so done.

Done with this decrepit reef. Done with this ragged life. Done lurking in the drowned remains of nobility, waiting for greedy men to stray from safe passage so she could bleed them of their cargo.

It paid her well. It kept her comfortable. But comfort was not luxury. Every haul, every scam, every drop of effort pulled her further from the throne she'd once deserved. Further from who she was meant to be.

"We'll punch through the hull mid-keel," Jetsam was saying.

"And while they're panicking, we take the loot," Flotsam finished.

"Brilliant," Ursula muttered flatly. "You'll do this in broad daylight, in open waters, with two dozen archers stationed on the top deck, harpoons at the ready. Remind me again, which one of you gets shot first?"

The eels exchanged a glance. Jetsam looked slightly less smug. Flotsam frowned, as though trying to do the math that would come up with the correct answer.

Sleek and bendy the eels were. Smart they were not.

"You want the bounty?" she continued, voice cool and low. "There's a smuggler's fog rolling in from the north reef by sunset. That's when you strike—silent, submerged. No fire. No show. Take the gold and let the ship continue on its way. They won't even know where the breach happened until they reach their trade destination."

"You make it sound so easy." Flotsam's tongue coiled around one of her nipples. The bud should've piqued. It remained flaccid.

"That's because I'm smarter than both of you combined." She brushed past him and reached for her seashell bra. This one was just a pale pink. It should not have gone with her flame red hair, but everything looked good on her. Even seaweed.

Ursula refastened the clasp of her seashell bra, fingers swift and practiced. The straps had rubbed raw at her shoulders after a day of slouching in salt and boredom. She adjusted the fit, smoothed her hair with a flick of her webbed fingers, and kept her back turned.

"That's a fair point about the fog," Flotsam murmured.

"What if we slip in from the undercurrent?" Jetsam said, already reworking her strategy like it had spawned fully formed from his own slippery mind. "Crack the haul from beneath while they're blind."

"Might even blame it on reef-rock," Flotsam said, a smirk in his tone. "Could make it look like an accident."

Ursula rolled her eyes so hard they nearly scraped the inside of her skull. Of course. That was how it always went. She'd feed them brilliance in pearls, and they'd spit it back at her in sand, grinning like they'd mined it themselves.

She didn't correct them. What was the point? Instead, she turned away from the ruin, her long fin slicing the water behind her like black silk.

"Where you off to, darling?" Jetsam asked.

"Out," she replied without looking back. "Someone's got to think further ahead than the next ship."

She was already halfway out of the ruins, gliding through a curtain of sea grass when the current shifted. The water trembled—an echo, a vibration. Something large slicing through the sea just above. She paused mid-stroke, instinct prickling along the ridges of her spine. The sea carried more than salt and shadow; it carried whispers, disturbances, danger. This one felt wrong.

Behind her, the coral reef dimmed as Flotsam and Jetsam darted past like arrows loosed from a bow.

"Ship," Jetsam hissed, giddy, vanishing into the gloom above.

Flotsam followed, his body curling around a jagged column of coral before surging toward the surface. "It's fast."

They all saw it at the same time.

The royal seal gleamed in the moonlight, stitched into its tattered sails—an ivory crest against deep navy fabric, flapping weakly in the breeze. The ship was lean and fast, built more for speed than cargo, but it moved strangely tonight—listing slightly, as if the current pulled against it or something inside had thrown it off balance.

"Leave it," Ursula commanded, her voice low, edged with warning.

Flotsam slithered ahead, his tail cutting through the dark like a knife. "It's a cutter. Easy pickings."

Ursula's fingers curled into fists, her nails biting into her palms. "That cutter is coming from the palace. What do they have to trade?"

"They might not have goods to trade," Jetsam whispered, voice slick as oil, "but they would have the means to trade with. Gold."

They were fools. Short-sighted, greedy fools. They didn't understand the balance of power, the delicate game of timing and precision she was playing. She had a plan—one that didn't involve petty theft or mindless destruction.

It was just like her brother. Just like her father. Men never listened—not unless she sang. Flotsam and Jetsam weren't worth wasting a song on. Neither were the humans worthy of saving.

She turned her back. But when she did, she heard a song. Low and guttural, it vibrated through the water like a war drum softened by distance. The melody wasn't woven with magic like her siren's call—it was rougher, a different pitch, an eel-song.

The sound coiled through the sea like a serpent, curling through trenches, wreckage, and forgotten caverns. It echoed off rusted hulls and the bones of long-dead leviathans. Flotsam and Jetsam didn't have the range to summon true monsters—but they didn't need to. They could call their allies from the deep.

A shimmer of bioluminescence flickered along the sea's floor—Glimmerscale Lanternfish, dozens of them, darting toward the ship above, casting illusions of lanterns, false beacons that would lure it straight into peril.

From the reef's edge, Gravecurrent Crabs lumbered into motion, their massive claws leaving trails in the silt. Barnacle-encrusted and armored with fragments of shipwrecks, they moved with eerie purpose, heading toward the ship's hull like siege engines rising from the grave.

Above, the ship still sailed, oblivious. Ursula turned back, her expression thunderous. "Fools. You'll tear everything down, and for what? A few pieces of gold?"

But her voice was swallowed by the chaos already rising around her. Dark shadows emerged from the depths, twisting, writhing, drawn by the call. Jagged fins cut through the water, gleaming rows of teeth flashed in the gloom, and the rhythmic pulsing of giant jellyfish sent eerie bioluminescence spiraling through the deep.

The monsters were awake. There was no stopping them now.

The crew's shouts rang out, loud and desperate, but they could do nothing against the horrors rising from below. Planks splintered. A mast snapped. Then, with a thunderous crack, the sea opened its mouth to swallow the ship whole.

The water churned with the wreckage of the ship, splintered wood and scattered cargo bobbing between overturned lifeboats. Distant cries echoed over the waves, voices thin and desperate against the vast stretch of sea. The scent of salt and burning pitch clung to the air, sharp and acrid, mixing with the bitter tang of blood.

Ursula drifted beneath it all, arms folded, watching

with cool detachment as the crew scrambled for safety. Pathetic creatures, humans. They clung to their fragile boats, their cargo forgotten, their desperate hands reaching for survival. Then he caught her eye.

A man—broad-shouldered, brown skin like fertile earth, strong, moving through the wreckage with purpose, not panic. Even here, amid chaos, he commanded. His voice cut through the shouts, firm and steady. And people listened.

Ursula did too. There was something about his voice. Something in the pitch of it.

She watched as he moved between the crew, hauling men to their feet, guiding them to lifeboats before stepping away to help the next. He didn't hesitate, didn't stop to think of himself first, didn't cling to a single scrap of cargo.

Idiot.

A fool who put others before himself, who thought that if he threw himself into the fire, someone might reach in to pull him out. No one would. No one ever did.

And then, as if the sea heard her thoughts, the mast gave way. A sharp crack split the air. The man had just helped the last sailor into a lifeboat when the towering mast collapsed, its rigging snapping like a giant's whip. The thick beam came crashing down, knocking him clean off his feet.

He hit the water hard, a burst of foam swallowing him whole. No one dove in after him. Not a single soul.

Ursula harrumphed, her lips pressing into a thin line. She could almost hear herself saying *I told you so.* She let herself sink, letting the sea cradle her as she peered through the gloom. Below the surface, the man drifted, ropes tangled around his limbs like hungry hands.

He wasn't struggling. A deep gash ran along his forehead. Dark blood curled into the water, mixing with the debris sinking around him. The hit had knocked him out. If the ropes didn't drown him, the weight of his own body would.

Ursula told herself it wasn't her problem. He had made his choice—to care, to save, to throw himself into the fray like a noble, self-sacrificing fool. And look where it got him.

Last time she saved someone, she'd lost her crown. She'd lost everything.

So what would this cost her?

With a frustrated flick of her tail, she surged forward, closing the distance between them in seconds. She would just put his head above water. That was it. She wasn't saving him.

She was simply… delaying the inevitable.

CHAPTER THREE

Eric felt like he was dreaming. It was the best dream he'd ever had. He was floating, weightless, adrift on a sea of warmth and silence. There was nothing to concern himself with. Nothing pulling at him. No burdens pressing on his shoulders.

The kingdom was fine. His mother was alive and nagging at him to finish his lessons. His father was strong, steady, the ruler Eric had once believed him to be, the ruler their people needed.

"Keep your head above the water."

The voice was not from the waking world. It was not from the dream, either. It was something divine in its clarity.

It was a woman's voice. Sweet would be the wrong word to describe it. It was more husky. It was commanding, warm like firelight and sharp like steel. He didn't know if it was memory or magic. But he obeyed.

His muscles screamed in protest as he fought his way upward. His limbs moved as though submerged, and the sea pulled at him. His head broke the surface, and air—blessed, raw, cutting air—filled his lungs in a gasping rush.

That was all he needed to do. Nothing else. Just breathe.

There were no other responsibilities here. No throne to worry about. No arranged marriages. No future looming like a storm on the horizon, ready to consume him whole.

All he had to do was be.

"Breathe," the voice demanded.

Right, and that. Eric did as he was told. Or he tried to. He wanted to please her. Somehow, he knew that it would please her if he followed her instructions.

He coughed, water pouring from his mouth and nose. He blinked against the sting of salt in his lungs and moonlight in his eyes. Or at least he thought his eyes were open.

Was he still dreaming? It had to be a dream. His mother was no longer on this earth with him. His father was off somewhere in the country, surrounding himself with sycophants and courtesans. His father was the reason Eric was all wet.

Why was Eric in the water? Because he'd gone to sea. Why had he gone to sea?

"Don't you dare die on me when I took the effort to save you."

She'd saved him. He wanted to say thank you. He wanted to save her right back. He was good at saving things, good at cleaning up messes. He wanted her to know that. He wanted this angel to come to depend on him. But first he had to get her in his line of sight.

And there she was. She was an angel. An angel with hair that was a wildfire of red, a flame untamed by wind or tide. Her eyes, impossibly blue, deeper than the sea, pierced through him. That smile—half amusement, half challenge, all annoyance—it stirred something in him, something restless and unfamiliar. Because it wasn't a smile. It was a smirk.

No woman had ever smirked at him like that, as though she expected him to prove himself worthy of her attention.

He liked that. He liked that she would make him work for it. He wanted to work for her attention. Once he caught her attention, he would bask in it forever.

Something shifted. Something burned in his chest. It was slow at first. Then searing, spreading like fire through his ribs.

A need. Desperate. All-consuming. Air. He needed more air.

"Breathe."

His mouth opened, but instead of a breath, his lungs filled with water, thick and heavy, choking him from the inside out.

The angel's smile faltered. She was yelling now, but he couldn't hear her words. Only her tone. She was furious.

Eric wanted to tell her not to frown. He wanted to reach for her, to keep her looking at him like that—not with worry, not with anger, but with that smirk, that spark, that challenge. He wanted her to believe in him again.

Then he heard a song. It was the most beautiful song he'd ever heard. He felt it thrum all through his body. It made him want to dance, to fly, to do everything she told him to do.

Breathe, she wanted him to breathe.

Eric coughed, his body seizing, rejecting the water in his lungs that had nearly claimed him. His chest expanded, air finally filling his reserves. Relief crashed over him. He gasped, drinking in the oxygen like a dying man, like he'd never had enough of it before.

The angel blurred. The warmth faded. This time, when he slipped back into the dream, there was no fire, no sea, no blue-eyed angel smiling at him.

There was only blackness.

Then a prick of light.

Then a raging fire.

The first thing Eric became aware of was the sound of Grimsby's voice—low, weary, and threaded with something he had never heard before. Worry.

"Come now, Your Highness. Don't drift away. Open your eyes."

Eric's eyelids felt too heavy, like he'd been pulled from somewhere far away, somewhere deeper than sleep. But he wanted to see her. If he opened his eyes, he would see her again. He was sure of it.

He forced them open, blinking against the warm glow of candlelight. The familiar scent of salt and aged wood filled the air, mixed with the faint traces of smoke from the fireplace and the lingering spice of old parchment. Thick velvet curtains had been drawn, blocking out the night, but through the small crack between them, he could see the moonlight spilling silver across the balcony.

He wasn't outside under the moonlight. He was in his bedroom. The room was grand but not extravagant, much like everything Eric allowed himself to have. A heavy wooden canopy bed, carved with intricate maritime designs, loomed over him. Maps and naval charts lined the walls, pinned beneath brass compasses and measuring tools. A broad desk sat near the window, usually cluttered with ledgers and unfinished notes, but now it held a tray of untouched food, a basin of water, and bloodied bandages.

He groaned, shifting against the crisp linens. There was a dull ache in his ribs. The lingering weight of exhaustion pressed down on him, keeping his back against the mattress.

Grimsby exhaled in relief, rubbing a hand over his lined face. He looked haggard.

Eric had never seen him like this before—always so put together, always so composed. Now his usually neat cravat was askew, and his coat looked like it had been thrown on in a hurry. There was a tightness to his features that made him look older.

"We thought we'd lost you." Grimsby's voice was quiet, but there was no mistaking the gravity in it.

It all came rushing back. The ship. The sudden churning of waves, as if the sea had turned against them. The monsters rising from the depths, teeth and tentacles and glowing eyes. The ship splitting apart, the sky tilting. The feeling of being dragged under. And then—her.

The red hair like wildfire. The piercing blue eyes. The smirk that dared him to fight. The voice that pulled him back. His chest tightened, his heart hammering with something that had nothing to do with the near-drowning.

"Is everyone safe?"

Grimsby nodded. "No lives were lost. The cutter was lost, but the liner made it out safe."

Eric let out a slow breath, relief easing some of the tension in his muscles. He closed his eyes for a brief second, but then blinked them open. He needed to know. He pushed himself up, ignoring the way his body protested. "Did you find her?"

Grimsby frowned. "Find who?"

"The girl." He'd wanted to say angel but thought better of it. "The one who rescued me."

"Your Highness, there was no one there when we found you. You washed ashore alone. You're lucky to be alive."

Alone? Eric's fingers curled against the sheets. Had he dreamed her?

The memory of her was so vivid, more real than any dream he'd ever had. He could still hear her voice—not words but sound, something deeper, something that had reached through the darkness and commanded him to live.

His mind could have invented that. But her face? That smirk? That wasn't something a man just imagined. Was it?

"Maybe I am."

But even as he said it, he wasn't sure if he meant lucky to be alive... or lucky to have seen her at all.

CHAPTER FOUR

The great coral doors of King Triton's court loomed before Ursula like a whale's mouth waiting to devour her whole. She entered with her proud head cast down as would a guppy seeking castoffs in the wake of a human's ship. It was demeaning, but she had very few choices these days. If there was one thing she could never be accused of, it was lacking audacity.

At her first opportunity, Ursula broke away from the school of simpering merpeople and sought her own path. She glided forward, her dark figure casting elongated shadows across the shimmering floor. She knew these halls like they were her own home because once upon a time they had been.

The once-familiar corridors seemed smaller now,

shrunken by time and her exile. Each twist and turn of the castle whispered memories she would rather forget. A snide comment from her father here, a rebuke from Triton there. The laughter of her cousins echoing in a chamber she had never quite belonged to. She had been allowed back for her father's burial in the deep sea but then promptly escorted out once again.

She swam deeper until the voices of the court grew faint. Finding herself before a door she hadn't seen in years, she brushed her fingers against its coral frame, and her lips curled into a sneer. This room had once been hers.

She eased the door open, slipping inside. The interior was unrecognizable. Gone were her elegant seashell furnishings and maps of the ocean floor. Instead, the space was cluttered, overflowing with an assortment of mismatched objects. Forks and candlesticks hung from seaweed strands like decorations. Rusted trinkets and chipped porcelain plates lined the walls.

Ursula's sneer deepened as she took it all in. The youngest princess, Ariel, had turned this room into an ode to her ridiculous obsession with the human world. Ariel's fascination with the air breathers bordered on sickness, as far as Ursula was concerned. What value could these crude, corroded baubles possibly hold?

The girl was never content with what was beneath

the waves. She had seen it for years—Ariel slipping away, breaking the surface, stepping onto human land like she had every right to be there, walking side by side with Princess Aurora, their laughter ringing out over the cliffs as they vanished into the golden spires of the human palace.

Ursula had saved Ariel from humans. Pulled the girl from the depths as her blood stained the sea. Torn the harpoon from her side and called a kraken to sink the humans who had dared to harm her.

And for what?

Ariel had repaid her with nothing but loss. Her father's trust. Her brother's… well, Triton had never done anything for Ursula. Her bedchamber had been taken. Her place in the kingdom stolen from her. She should have let the sea claim the brat that day.

Ursula exhaled sharply, forcing herself to push the thought of Ariel aside. She had wasted enough time regretting saving one fool—why had she gone and saved another today?

She hadn't meant to. She had watched the man sink, bound in ropes, left behind by the very men he had tried to save. He had fought for them, dragged them into lifeboats, put their lives above his own, and in the end—not a single one had come for him.

He was a fool. Just like her.

She had once believed in loyalty, had fought for

something greater than herself, had risked everything for family, for duty, for the love of her people—and what had it gotten her?

Exile. Betrayal. A life spent scavenging instead of ruling.

She had learned her lesson. Hopefully, he had learned his. If he survived. She was sure he would. A bright light like his.

Something inside her hadn't wanted to see that light die out. She had seen the way he moved, the way the crew listened when he spoke, the way he had not hesitated to throw himself into the fire for the sake of others.

It was stupid. Reckless. Weak.

And still, she had reached for him. She would never see that sailor again. He was not her concern.

What was her concern was her empty pockets. With the mess Flotsam and Jetsam had made of the royal ship, they'd let the liner that had likely been carrying the gold slip by them. All of her carefully laid plans, instead of sinking to the bottom of the sea's floor for easy pickings, were now out to sea. It would be days, possibly weeks, before the liner returned, if they were smart.

Ursula swam past a pile of tarnished silverware and stopped at a vanity adorned with pearls and aquamarine. Her gaze locked on a small chest half-buried beneath a tangle of nets. Flipping it open, Ursula smiled. Inside was a collection of gleaming jewels— emeralds, sapphires, rubies, all shimmering like captured starlight.

Her fingers lingered on a particularly large sapphire. This stone had belonged to their grandmother. It had been passed down to Ursula, but Triton hadn't allowed her to take it with her when he'd banished her. She tightened her grip.

It wasn't thievery. Not that Ursula had a problem with taking anything from the royal family. These jewels were her birthright. She slipped the chain around her neck and tucked the gem inside one of her seashells. The sapphire warmed her breast as she pulled the cloak back over her head. With one last glance at the chaotic space, she slipped back into the hallway.

A shadow passed over the corridor ahead. Ursula froze, shrinking into the corner as a patrol of guards approached. One of them paused, sniffing the water into his gills.

"Did you hear something?"

The other guard yawned. "Probably just a crab."

Ursula rolled her eyes. She could almost pity her brother for ruling over such imbeciles. Almost.

The guards lumbered past. Ursula resumed her escape, only to pause again when she turned the next corner. There, standing at the far end of the hall, was Triton himself.

Her big brother was the only one who could see through her illusions. No matter how carefully she masked her appearance, her brother's piercing eyes would always find her. Luckily, he was distracted now.

King Triton stood at the edge of the coral dais, his massive frame coiled with tension. Muscles corded along his arms as he gripped his golden trident—a weapon of legend, crackling faintly with restrained power. His sea-blue eyes were stormy, his heavy brow furrowed beneath the weight of his crown. Salt-crusted strands of silver hair floated around his head like a mane, giving him the appearance of a sea god carved from wrath and stone. The long sweep of his tail, opalescent and edged with a sharp fin, flicked restlessly as he paced.

Before him hovered a much smaller figure. Sebastian stood upright on two jointed legs, the carapace of his shell polished to a lacquered red gleam. His pincers tapped together with an anxious rhythm, and his eyestalks twitched as he tried to keep pace with the king's agitation.

"She's still missing?"

"Yes, Your Majesty." Sebastian's voice carried the clipped, proper cadence of someone used to bearing bad news—and the bite of royal tempers.

Triton's grip on his trident tightened. "I want every current searched."

"Yes, sire." Sebastian bowed low, though his voice muttered under his breath, "As if we haven't already turned the ocean inside out…"

Triton didn't hear. Or perhaps he did and simply chose not to respond. His gaze had already drifted, scanning the endless blue as if sheer force of will might summon his wayward daughter back to him.

Of course, it was Ariel that was missing. All of her sisters were bound to other mermen in different seas across the world. Each one an alliance that merged the waterways under Triton's command. It was Ariel, the youngest and the most spoiled, who thought she could do as she pleased and go wherever she fancied.

"I don't understand why the princess keeps disappearing," said a lady's maid whom Ursula somewhat recognized. The woman had been in attendance to her when she was the jewel of the crown.

"It's likely bridal nerves," suggested another. "She's set to meet her betrothed tomorrow."

Betrothed? So big brother had gone and gotten his last daughter on a hook. Ursula wondered with which sea.

"This alliance with the King of the Coastlands is vital," barked her brother.

The Coastlands? That was no sea. So that was the

price of peace? Ursula had wondered how her father and brother had gotten the Coastal King to cave. Now she knew.

If she hadn't have been banished, would that have been her fate? An arranged marriage to the Prince of the Coast? Better Ariel than her. Ursula had no interest in being any man's pawn.

"Send out a search party. We cannot afford a delay. My daughter must meet Prince Eric at the docks tomorrow morning or the trading agreement could collapse. This alliance is vital to the kingdom. She must be present. Sebastian, go and stall the prince while the guards search."

Poor, precious Ariel. So adored, so sheltered—and so utterly incapable of handling the pressures of royal life.

Ursula had tried to warn her father. She'd told him that Triton's guppies didn't have the mettle to rule. And what had she gotten for her troubles? Passed over by her father and banished by her brother.

Well, this was them all getting their just desserts.

"Princess Ariel?"

Ursula froze for half a heartbeat before her lips curled into an amused grin. The guard's mistake was delicious. She and Ariel shared the same dark hair and sharp features. The resemblance had always been uncanny—a source of bitterness during her years in the court.

The guard frowned, confusion creeping into his gaze as he looked closer. "Wait... you're not—"

Before he could finish, Ursula straightened, her voice taking on a low, hypnotic hum as she began to sing. "You saw nothing," she said, her words rippling through the water, melodic and irresistible. "You will not go out to look for the princess. You will go and get drunk instead. Do you understand?"

The guard's expression went slack, his earlier suspicion dissolving under the weight of her siren's song. "Get... drunk."

Ursula smiled, her teeth glinting in the dim light. "Good boy. Now off you go."

The guard swam past her, dazed but determined, his earlier mistake already forgotten.

Ursula lingered in the corridor, her mind alight with a new idea. For too long, she'd been reduced to sneaking around these waters that should've been hers. She'd been the one that had to go around hiding who she was to survive.

That would all stop. She would sneak onto the coast and meet the human prince face to face. It would be her face that he looked upon. But it would be Ariel's name that she gave him.

She flexed her fingers, power crackling faintly in the

water around her. Ariel was missing. Triton was desperate. The prince was expecting a wide-eyed, innocent princess—but what he'd get was someone far more cunning.

With a dark laugh, Ursula slipped into the depths, her plan fully formed. By the time she surfaced, she would no longer be the outcast sister. She would be married to the prince and return to her throne as queen.

CHAPTER FIVE

The morning sun burned too brightly. Its golden light slanted through the high-arched windows of the palace halls, warming the polished stone floors beneath Eric's boots. Outside, the sea stretched calm and endless. The waves were gentler than his thoughts as they rolled toward the shore in a steady rhythm.

Today was the day he was supposed to meet his future wife. He should have felt restless. He should have been preparing. Instead, Eric's mind drifted back to *her*—a woman who did not exist.

The dream had burrowed into him, lingering in ways he didn't understand. He saw her face every time he closed his eyes. He felt the way she had looked at him—not with reverence, not with duty, but with challenge.

Those crystal blue eyes hadn't challenged him to live. They'd dared him to defy her. He wanted to laugh. He did, a low chuckle that was more desire than amusement.

For the first time in his life, Eric, the Prince of the Coastlands, had wanted something just for himself. It was a good thing his dream girl wasn't real. Because if she had been, he would have seriously considered shirking his duties. That thought unsettled him more than any shipwreck ever could.

All of these duties to run the kingdom should have belonged to the king—his father. But the man hadn't been a ruler in years. Eric liked to believe his father was grieving. The truth was he'd simply given up and then given in to his vices.

Five years ago, the queen had gone to sleep for the last time. The once-vibrant king had begun to rot from the inside out. Grief gave way to gambling. Guilt to gluttony. The crown remained on his father's head, but the weight of it had shifted—onto Eric's back.

At an age when most young men were still finding their footing, Eric had been forced to wear his father's boots. He balanced the books while his father spent lavishly. He sat on the throne to resolve disputes between bickering merchants and land-hungry nobles.

When the navy faltered, it was Eric who oversaw their patrol routes. He hadn't even been of age to serve, but they'd handed him the reins of the military like the birthright it was instead of a burden.

And he had done it all. Without a word of complaint. Even as it cracked his spine and ground down his youth. Even when the council came to him with the treaty his father had signed, asking—no, expecting—him to marry a foreign princess he'd never met. A woman who wasn't even human.

He'd said yes. Of course he'd said yes. Because Eric knew his duty. Because his kingdom came first. Because someone had to care.

But today...

Today, something shifted.

For the first time in his life, Eric, the Prince of the Coastlands, had wanted something just for himself. A selfish, reckless, impossible thing. A girl from a dream. A phantom with eyes like the sea and lips that tasted like freedom.

She'd breathed life back into his lungs. He hadn't been awake for it, but he'd been conscious of it. It was what his mind clung to as death squeezed him in its grip. What his heart listened to as it regained its rhythm.

She had been a phantom, maybe even a figment of his imagination. But she had felt so real.

A sharp, irritated voice from the corridor snapped him out of his thoughts. Eric turned toward the commotion just as Grimsby entered the chamber, pinching the bridge of his nose, his usual restraint clearly fraying. Behind him, a sea emissary followed.

Sebastian's hard crimson shell gleamed in the morning light, his bug-like eyes bulging, darting around the room. His clawed hands tapped out a quick, staccato rhythm against his own forearm, an anxious, impatient *click-click-click*.

Eric had encountered sea folk many times before. They had free rein in the market, trading alongside humans, fae, and shifters alike. But there was something particularly animated about this creature.

Grimsby exhaled sharply, straightening his coat as he approached. "Your Highness, it seems we have a delay."

Eric raised an eyebrow. "A delay?"

"The princess's arrival has been… postponed."

There was a beat of silence.

Eric knew he should feel annoyance. He should be irritated, should be concerned about what it meant for the alliance, should be wondering what message this sent—whether the Sea Kingdom was playing politics or simply being careless.

Instead—relief. It flooded through him before he

could stop it, before he could remind himself of what was at stake, what was expected of him.

Maybe... maybe it wasn't a slight. Maybe it wasn't political maneuvering at all. Maybe it was the princess who was having second thoughts.

The idea bloomed quietly in his chest, lifting some of the heaviness he'd been carrying. Not because he wanted her to break the deal—they still needed this treaty. Because dream or not, he didn't want to start his marriage by clinging to another woman in his thoughts. Even if that woman had only existed in the depths of a dream... or was it a memory?

He still wasn't sure.

He could still feel the press of her fingertips on his skin. The salt-slick warmth of her hair tangled in his hands. The softness of her voice—like wind against sails or the hush of the sea at dawn—whispering for him to hold on, to live.

He didn't know if he had imagined her. But he did know he wasn't ready to let thoughts of her go just yet. Just a few more days. A few more days to bask in the memory—or the fantasy—before duty claimed him again.

Once it did, he would bury her. He would forget her. Because that was what a good ruler, a good husband, did.

Sebastian's claws snapped together sharply, pulling

Eric's attention back to the emissary. "I assure you, the princess is most eager to meet her betrothed, but certain… ah… unforeseen circumstances have delayed her departure."

Eric wasn't foolish enough to ask for details. The Sea Kingdom kept their secrets tightly wound beneath the waves. He clasped his hands behind his back, forcing a composed expression. "I'm sure whatever has delayed her is… important."

Grimsby cleared his throat, as if willing Eric to at least pretend at disappointment.

"I only wish for her to arrive safely. That is my first concern." A non-answer, perfectly diplomatic. Eric was back on his game. "Can we offer you some hospitality? I would be grateful if you dined with us."

The crab clicked his claws again and took a step back. "Dinner at a human table does not sound appetizing. I will return to search for—I mean seek out an arrival date for your betrothed."

Eric nodded, as was expected. But he had caught the slip. Something was wrong.

The moment the crab was gone, Grimsby let out a long-suffering sigh. "My spies tell me that the princess has not been seen in the Sea Kingdom for some days."

"Do you think she's run away?"

"It would be bad if she did. We need this alliance."

Eric tamped down on the rising relief. This was his duty.

"I've taken the liberty to send out some of our men to look for the princess as well. It's a quietly kept secret that she has a *friendship* with Princess Aurora."

Eric didn't understand why Grimsby put emphasis on the word. Princess Aurora was everything a princess of the realm should be. It was good that she and the mermaid were amiable.

"Aurora is set to marry Prince Phillip soon."

Eric had met Phillip before and liked the man immensely. Phillip and Aurora were two very different people, but that was royal marriages for you. It wasn't about personal preferences. It was all about alliances and agreements. It would make sense that Aurora and Ariel would befriend each other, as both women were facing the same fates. He hoped the two forged a deep bond. He certainly wouldn't get in the way of their friendship moving forward.

"I'm going to head to the docks."

"Not another sea voyage," moaned Grimsby.

"Just need to stretch my legs after being in bed all day."

"You were in bed all night like a normal person. Likely the first full night's sleep you've had in years."

"Yes, and it's made me restless. I won't be long."

"Just promise to come back. I can't have two royal runaways on my hands."

Running away from his duties was something Eric had never considered. At least not before the dream of red hair and sea-blue eyes. But he didn't have to run away from that vision. He simply needed to go somewhere alone, close his eyes, and revel in a dream that would never come true.

CHAPTER SIX

The waters near the shore were different from the deep—warmer, saltier, carrying the scent of sunbaked sand and the musk of human civilization. Ursula swam just beneath the surface, her dark form slicing through the current like a shadow. The weight of her plan pressed against her shoulders like the crushing depths of the sea.

She was going to impersonate Ariel. The thought coiled in her gut like a slick, unwelcome eel. She would have to play the part—silent, simpering, sweet. It was going to be infuriating.

All her life, her father and brother had refused to hear her voice—cut her off, dismissed her, silenced her. But when it suited them? Oh, then they'd pluck her words like pearls from the sea floor, polish them, present them as their own. Her ideas, her strategies, her brilliance—all stolen, twisted into decrees proclaimed from a throne she was born to serve but never allowed to approach.

Her father would've married her off like Triton had done with his daughters, traded away like shiny trinkets for treaties with distant oceans and far-off seas. But both of them knew Ursula was too mouthy, too head-strong, too disobedient to bend to any sea creature's will. She'd have burned the bridal reef down before letting herself be used as a pawn.

So when the excuse came—when one tiny ripple of scandal, one surge of power she hadn't properly bowed for, made the court shift nervously—they pounced. They snared the moment like hunters in bloodied water, and they cast her off. Banished her from the palace, from the family, from the kingdom she had been born to shape.

And since then? The kingdom had dulled.

Once, the Sea Kingdom had led the tides—bold, thriving, admired. Now they clung to crumbling coral and outdated customs. Instead of leading the waves, they were falling behind the wake. The other seas were advancing, evolving. But not hers. No, these waters were struggling to stay relevant. Groveling for alliances with landlocked humans and inland kings just to stay afloat.

Sea creatures struggling to keep their heads above water. The shame of it. They wouldn't be simpering to surface-dwellers if she still had a voice in court. If her ideas hadn't been swept away like wreckage. If they hadn't cast out their most cunning daughter for saving the life of a brat.

And wasn't that the cruelest irony of all? That now she was slinking toward human royalty, courting the very creatures her father had always loathed, pretending she had no voice—just to take back what was hers. Fate had a cruel sense of humor.

Ariel had never known this kind of silence. The youngest princess had been born without a voice box, never able to shape words, never able to argue or demand. And for a fleeting, strange moment, Ursula felt something almost like pity—a flicker of tragedy in the fact that Ariel would never know what it was like to be truly heard.

But Ursula knew that pain. She had lived it. And Ariel—spoiled, indulged, adored Ariel—had never suffered for it. Even without a voice, she had commanded attention, had learned how to manipulate without words, had basked in her father's love while Ursula was cast out.

The flicker of pity was snuffed out as quickly as it had come. Ariel had never been silent. She had been a demanding, whining, ever-present reminder that Ursula had been pushed aside, forgotten, stripped of her rightful place. But now Ariel would serve a purpose.

Ursula smirked, tilting her head back as she floated beneath the skies. The gentle lap of waves against the rocky shore was almost soothing. Let them all ignore her now. By the time she was done, she wouldn't need to speak. She would have everything she was owed.

She had almost reached the shore when she spotted them. A small delegation of sea folk waded into the shallows, their forms eerie and shifting beneath the waves. At their head was Sebastian, his hard crimson shell gleaming, his bug-like eyes darting nervously from side to side as though he expected an ambush at any moment.

Ursula curled her fingers into the sand, her claws raking through the silty seabed. She couldn't be seen. She eased herself deeper into the shadows, letting the seaweed sway around her like a cloak. The salty brine thickened the air around her, mixing with the faint scent of fish and decay from the tide pools clinging to the shore.

Sebastian let out a frustrated click of his claws, his

tone sharp, strained. "This will not work forever. Prince Eric—he is no fool."

A ripple of unease passed through the small group. One of the diplomats, a tall, sleek creature with dark, shining scales, flicked his fins impatiently. "The princess will be found. We just need more time."

Sebastian scoffed, his clawed hands tapping out a rapid click-click-click against his own shell. "Time? Time?! We don't have time. Did you hear the latest report? A royal ship went down the other night."

"The reports are that it was in unsanctioned waterways. We have warned the humans about going beyond our protection."

"What if they start to think we can't protect them even in those waters?" Sebastian shot back. "With Ariel missing, what if they think we can't control our own princess? The humans are restless, the treaty is unstable. If we do not get this marriage finalized, we risk losing the alliance entirely."

"We just need to keep Prince Eric believing that she's simply… delayed. If he suspects the truth—"

"Then the whole thing falls apart," Sebastian finished grimly.

Silence fell over the group, heavy as the tide. The moment Sebastian and his delegation slipped beneath the waves, Ursula pulled herself onto a jagged rock, the wet stone rough and barnacle-bitten beneath her palms. She flicked her tail against the rock, watching the way the scales gleamed, still slick from the sea.

A pressure built behind her ribs, a bone-deep ache, like her very body resisted what she was asking it to become. Her spine arched as the transformation took hold. The silver-blue of her scales dulled, the iridescence fading into vulnerable skin. Her tail split, slowly, painfully, like a flower forced to bloom through frost. Muscles stretched in unfamiliar ways. Nerves sparked to life. Flesh reshaped and bones groaned as they reformed—knees, calves, feet—until what had once been fin was now a leg.

She collapsed onto her side with a gasp, her breath ragged. Cool air kissed the insides of her thighs—skin that hadn't felt wind in years. She was completely bare from the waist down and shivering. The water still clung to her, salt drying sticky against her skin, her hair plastered to her back and shoulders.

When she finally pushed herself upright, her arms trembled under her weight. Her legs were unsteady beneath her, the muscles foreign, too long unused. She managed to stand, one foot, then the other, wobbling like a newborn foal. Each step was a negotiation between gravity and grace.

But still—she was up. On land. The sun cut through a break in the clouds and kissed her damp skin, warming the gooseflesh there. Somewhere in the distance, a gull screamed.

Ursula tilted her chin up to the sky, her mouth twisting into a smile not of joy but triumph. Now all she had to do was sneak into the palace and become the princess they were so desperately waiting for. She could already picture it—draped in silk, smiling sweetly, nodding like a well-mannered fool while Eric fell right into her hands. She'd bat her lashes, play the docile little thing the kingdom expected, all while securing the power that had always been meant for her.

Ariel had run away. Ursula was going to walk right into her place. She took a steady step forward—and froze. Because someone was watching her.

She felt it before she saw it—that prickle along her spine, the deep, wordless awareness of eyes upon her. Slowly, too slowly, she lifted her gaze. And there he was.

The man she had pulled from the sea.

The man she had almost let drown.

The one she should have forgotten.

He stood on the shore, dark hair tousled from the wind. Beneath a dark cloak, his white shirt was open at the collar, sleeves rolled up to his forearms. The white was stark against his brown skin. His eyes were locked on to her.

Not with fear.

Not with suspicion.

With recognition.

A strange, unexpected current ran through her. Her pulse jumped, but her expression didn't flicker. They simply stared at each other.

Then, slowly, his lips parted. "It's you. You're Ariel."

CHAPTER SEVEN

From the moment Eric had spotted her red hair—striking even from the distance of the cliff—he'd known. That was the woman who had saved him. He hadn't dreamed it. She was real.

She emerged from the water like an ancient goddess, as if the sea itself had crafted her from foam and salt and offered her up to the sun. His breath had caught in his chest, but that was the only part of his body that had stalled.

He picked up his pace, boots slipping on the uneven path as he made his way down the rocky incline. His heartbeat thundered in his ears, drowning out the crash of waves. He meant to call out, to hail her, but then he saw the flicker of movement in the waves—a fin, a shimmer of scales—and the Sea Kingdom delegation not far off, sliding back beneath the surface.

She was hiding from them.

He ducked low, instinctively crouching behind the rocks, just in time to see her pull herself up onto a jagged outcrop, the water cascading off her tail in rivulets of silver and blue. The sight of her mermaid form—real and not the fanciful sketches from old books—left his mouth dry, the humid sea air doing nothing to ease the sudden burn in his throat. Then her body began to change.

Eric stared, awestruck, helpless. Her transformation wasn't graceful. It was raw, powerful, almost painful to witness. Her tail split, scaled limbs stretching into legs, knees drawing up to her chest as the magic reshaped her. Skin replaced shimmer. A woman emerged from the sea's embrace, trembling and magnificent.

And she was completely, utterly naked from the waist down.

Eric turned so fast he nearly stumbled. Heat rushed to his face. Mortification and desire clashed in his chest like dueling swords. It was the honorable thing to do to grant her privacy. But every instinct in him screamed to look back.

Not for lust. Not this time. He was afraid if he blinked, she'd vanish again.

He stole a glance over his shoulder. She stood

unsteadily on the slick rocks. Her red hair was plastered to her spine. The sunlight gilded every curve of her body. Her arms were out for balance, her bare feet unsure on land.

She looked fragile. Vulnerable. Human.

But he knew the truth. This was her. Ariel. His intended bride.

Nothing about this moment felt arranged or dutiful. She wasn't a stranger from the Sea Kingdom. She was the girl who had pulled him from death, who haunted his dreams and now stood before him in the flesh.

She was the dream. She was the most beautiful thing he had ever seen. And she was intended for him.

Prince Eric of the Coastlands forgot himself. Forgot his name, his rank, the fact that he was standing on the shore like a man caught between a dream and waking.

She looked up. Their eyes met. A flicker of startled recognition flashed across her face—then wariness.

She was running from her father. Did that mean she was running from Eric, too? But she'd saved him. He must mean something to her. She at least didn't want him dead.

It was a start. He just needed to charm her. But he'd never charmed a woman in his life. He'd been too busy with matters of state to focus on courtiers.

"It's you. You're Ariel."

Stating the obvious seemed like a good start. It was,

at the very least, safer than saying *You're the most beautiful thing I've ever seen, and I can't feel my legs.*

Her name tasted right in his mouth. She didn't deny it. They had an agreed-upon foundation in this meeting.

"I'm Prince Eric of the Coastlands. Your father and mine arranged an alliance years ago. You and I are to be married."

She quirked a brow at this. That brow quirk read *You're stating the obvious.* But at least she didn't run away from him like she had with her father or hide like she had with the sea delegation. Eric was counting it as a win.

He cleared his throat again, straightened his spine, and forced himself into the posture of a man negotiating borders instead of standing before a naked sea princess with legs that had only just learned how to walk.

"We don't know each other. Obviously. But I thought—since you saved my life—that maybe we could... start there. As a foundation. A... negotiation."

Her lips parted. She said nothing.

"You saved me. So I'm in your debt. If you're running from your father, I can offer you sanctuary. A place to stay. No pressure."

Ariel tilted her head, bemused. She didn't look

frightened. Or angry. Just amused. Her mouth twitched like she was suppressing a laugh.

"You're not running from me," he said softly. "That's good. Because I'd really like to keep you."

Her sea-blue eyes flashed at him like a cat's. It was a reminder that he was in the presence of someone who was not quite human. She was a siren. She could bend him to her will with a note.

She said nothing. She was also wearing nothing except a bejeweled set of clamshells over her breasts and a sapphire resting on her chest.

Eric shrugged off his cloak then removed his shirt. The cotton fabric was still warm from his body as he pulled it over his head. His movements were quick, efficient—anything to keep from looking at her again. He stepped forward, holding it out.

"Take this."

She didn't move at first. Just watched him, her blue eyes unreadable, the morning sun turning them to liquid fire. Then, slowly, she reached out and took the shirt from his hands.

Her fingers brushed his. The contact sent a sharp jolt up his arm. Eric swallowed hard, stepping back as she pulled the fabric over her shoulders. It hung loosely on her frame, too large, the sleeves slipping past her wrists. The sight of his clothing on her body made something tighten low in his stomach.

"We don't have to tell them you're here. That I found you. It can be our secret."

She studied him. Eric puffed up his chest, wanting to preen like a peacock for her. He raised his hands and began making the signs he'd learned that she communicated with.

Why did you run?

Once again, he'd caught her off guard. Her lips parted… instead of raising her hands to answer, words came out of her mouth. "You learned sign language?"

"Apparently unnecessarily."

She pursed her lips. He wanted to know why she chose not to speak. Was it another power play? Was it her idea or her father's?

"Were you running from your kingdom? Or mine?"

She pursed her lips again, but this time she was clearly studying him. She was going to answer him, but Eric wasn't done.

"Is it because you're unsure of me? If so, I understand. I was unsure of you. Until just a moment ago, when I realized you were the same woman who rescued me from the sea."

She clutched the collar of his shirt closer to her neck. Eric wanted to replace the fabric with his mouth.

"Talk to me. Tell me what you need."

Her eyes glazed over in a pleasure-filled way. She

swayed a bit. Toward him. He had never felt more like a man than in that moment.

"Is that what you need? Do you need me to rescue you?"

Something flickered in her eyes at the word rescue —something that didn't sit right. Her lashes lowered, slowly and deliberately, a coy flutter that was clearly meant to charm. Somehow, he knew that this wasn't her. The look was too practiced, too demure. False, somehow. Like a costume that didn't quite fit.

Eric felt the instinct to step back. He had an uncomfortable sense that she'd put on a mask for him. And he didn't want the mask. He wanted her.

"Yes, my prince. I need you to rescue me from my villainous father."

Eric ignored the prickle at the back of his neck. He offered Ariel his arm. This was what he was good at. He was good at taking charge, taking care of people. He would prove to his bride that he could protect her. But first, he needed to convince her that she needed to become his bride.

CHAPTER EIGHT

The moment the prince's eyes fell on her, Ursula knew—this would be easy.

His gaze flickered, dropped, then dragged back up, like a man caught between temptation and duty. Like a man whose body was betraying him even while his mind begged him to look away. Men were so simple. All she needed to do was get him into bed, make him crave her touch, and he would belong to her completely.

She had played this game before, had used her voice, her body to lure fools into her grasp. She knew how to play the damsel, how to let her lips tremble just so, how to widen her eyes in feigned innocence, how to shiver in a man's presence and make him think she needed saving. Men were helpless to come to the rescue—at least, men of power were.

The weak ones, the Flotsams and Jetsams of the world, the creatures that slithered in the dark, they weren't interested in saving anything. They only knew how to take, how to leech power from someone stronger. The eels' powers combined made for an interesting dive in the seaweed, sure. Outside of a bed of seaweed, they thrived on fear, on desperation, on having someone else to prey on.

Men like Prince Eric? The ones raised to command? Those brought up to lead, to carry the burdens of others? They were helpless to resist the helpless. They wanted to be needed.

Ursula would wager the prince was a mama's boy.

"Take me back to your castle," she said, feigning breathlessness, letting herself sound like a girl lost, fragile, in need of a strong protector. "Keep me safe from my father and his goons."

Prince Eric pursed his lips. There were prickles of light in his hazel eyes. He was not quite under her spell. He looked like he was thinking. With the brain closer to the sun than the one nearer to the sea.

"No," he said. "That's not the best idea."

Irritation flashed through Ursula like lightning. He wasn't listening to her. He'd brushed her words, her wants, her plan aside for his desires.

She'd been all wrong about him the other day when she'd saved him. Wrong about whatever she thought she'd seen in his eyes. Wrong about the man who had saved all those lives at a cost to his own. He had been stupid to put others in front of himself. And now he would try to put himself in front of her.

"If I take you to the castle, someone from the court will let your father know you are here. Or they'll, at the least, let my father know, and that man holds secrets as well as he holds his spirits. No, I have a better idea. We wait until nightfall. In the meantime, we go to the market and get you something to eat."

"Something to… eat?"

"You must be famished. When's the last time you ate? How long have you been running? Or rather swimming?" He glanced down at her bare legs, then blinked as though caught leering. "Let's get you taken care of. Get food in your belly. Clothes on your back. Let's get you off those feet. I'm told walking is taxing for merkind. Would you like me to carry you?"

"I…carry me?"

He pulled his arms back, hands up as though she was a guard about to put him under arrest. "Did I overstep?"

"No… You… I can walk."

Eric smiled, as if pleased with himself. He lowered one arm and offered her the other. Just as she reached for it, he hesitated. His gaze searched hers, something shifting in his expression. Those sparkling thought bubbles dimmed, focusing in on her.

"Do you disagree with my plan, my lady?"

Ursula's mind short-circuited, sparks firing in all directions in searching for the right response. She'd never been asked this question before. She'd always had to be the one to carry the heaviest load.

"Tell me what you want and I'll give it to you."

Her lips parted, and the truth fell out like an anchor sinking into the deep. "I want to sit on a throne."

Silence.

And then—he smiled. Not the soft, comforting smile of a prince indulging a girl's wishes. It was the look of a man intrigued, as if she had just told him his cock was the biggest she'd ever encountered.

Of course, she would tell him that when he presented said cock to her. Right now he stood before her, wearing a cocksure grin.

Prince Eric's fingers curled gently around her wrist, pulling her just a fraction closer. "After I feed and clothe you, you can sit on mine. Would you like that?"

Ursula's thoughts tangled like seaweed in a riptide. It had to be the salt in the air. She wasn't sure if they were talking about an actual chair or his lap. She wasn't sure which she wanted more at this moment.

A shiver ran down her spine, down the backs of her legs, and out to her toes. It was an unfamiliar experience, not just because she rarely used her legs or feet. For the first time in her life, someone wasn't trying to quiet her. Someone was listening to her.

Prince Eric's eyes searched her face, hesitant, considering. He was still holding her hand, his grip firm, steady. His expression had shifted. He regarded her as if something about her didn't quite fit.

Ursula wasn't used to males trying to figure her out. She was used to being admired for her beauty. Men revered softness, obedience, a woman's willingness to follow. They didn't look at her like this—like she was something capable, something to be reckoned with.

"I didn't thank you for rescuing me," he said.

Instead of responding, Ursula demurred. What was she supposed to say? That it was a lapse in judgment? That he'd caught her in a weak moment? She lowered her gaze and let him read into that what he would.

"You put yourself in danger when you did. You could've been seen, either by my men or by others from the sea. You must be very cunning to evade the entire might of the sea army."

It was on the tip of her tongue to agree, to confirm just how clever, just how shrewd, just how utterly untouchable she was. Because she was. But that was her as Ursula. Not as Ariel.

Ursula swallowed down her pride, masking her emotions with a small, practiced smile, keeping her gaze cast downward as if embarrassed by the compliment.

Prince Eric's arm was solid beneath her touch. The muscles flexing under her splayed fingers resting in the crook of his elbow. She noted the strength there, the way he moved with effortless control.

A wild, ridiculous thought slid into her mind: *If I put all my weight on him, would he carry me?* The idea was so absurd, so unlike her, that she snuffed it out immediately.

CHAPTER NINE

"Fresh-caught mackerel, served raw and sliced thin, as madam requested," the chef announced as he set the plate before the disguised sea princess. "With a side of sea grapes and raw shrimp, lightly brushed with lime brine and a dusting of crushed coral salt. And for His Highness"—he turned with a flourish, setting down the second plate—"slow-roasted boar, rubbed in mountain thyme and coastal fennel, served over sweetroot mash with a drizzle of honeyed glaze. Your drinks—sea lavender tea for the lady, crisp and floral, and a dark berry cordial for you, sire. Tart with just enough bite to cut the richness. Enjoy your meal."

Eric nodded politely, but the chef's words barely

registered. He couldn't take his eyes off her. Ariel sat across from him at a small wooden table beneath the awning of a café, eating with a hunger that was both unapologetic and mesmerizing. Eric's gaze lingered on her mouth, on the way her lips glistened as she licked a drop of brine from the corner, on the delicate movement of her throat as she swallowed.

The marketplace swirled around them, sun-drenched and vibrant. The smells of roasting meats and citrus drifted through the air. Children laughed near a fountain. Coins clinked. Somewhere, a fiddler played a jaunty tune that had the foot-tappers and skirt-spinners gathering in rhythm. None of it registered next to the beauty within Eric's arm span.

He could reach out and touch her. He could taste her lips—she was to be his bride, after all. Instead, he bided his time.

The sea princess had asked for nothing. Well, nothing he wasn't already prepared to give her. She wanted to rule next to him on his throne. She'd been eager to cast off his cotton shirt—that had irked him. But then she'd happily donned the silk gown he'd purchased for her. He should have bought her seashells, pearls, gems. But the silk highlighted her curves so well.

She wasn't the princess he had heard about in rumors—the delicate, fragile thing raised in the shadow of her father. There was a strength to her, a toughness that he hadn't expected. She knew her own mind. She didn't yield to fear. She carried herself like she owned the world.

Eric took a slow sip of his drink, watching her, trying to piece together the contradiction of it all. She must have hidden a part of herself her entire life, just as he had. Forced to be what her kingdom needed, like him. But here, now, together—they didn't have to be. Here, they were just a man and a woman, sitting in the sun, sharing a meal, speaking of nothing and every-thing, belonging only to each other.

He didn't want to go back to the castle. Didn't want to return to the suffocating walls of duty, expectation, obligation. Not yet. Not when this moment was solely about the two of them.

Ariel clearly wasn't used to sitting in a dress because the way she sat showed off a little too much leg. Others noticed. Eric saw them—the way a pair of men nearby let their eyes linger too long, their gazes sliding over her like they had a right to look.

A slow, dangerous heat curled in his chest. Before he even realized what he was doing, a low growl rumbled in his throat. It was a warning, and it was effective. The men startled, eyes snapping away as quickly as they had dared to look.

Satisfied, Eric turned back to Ariel—only to find her watching him. Amusement shone bright in her sea-blue gaze. Her lips curled into a knowing grin.

She had seen everything. She wasn't blushing at his show of possession. She looked pleased by his show of aggression.

On her plate, nestled beside the shimmering slices of raw mackerel was a small mound of live shrimp. Their translucent bodies wiggled with life. Their legs twitched in the shallow pool of citrus-laced seawater.

The sea princess plucked a wriggling morsel from the wooden plate, its translucent tendrils curling in protest. She popped it between her lips, chewing slowly, savoring every bite. "Are you disgusted?"

"I doubt anything you do could disgust me. I just… You'd rather not have it cooked?"

"There's no fire in the sea. We don't eat dead things."

She picked up another wriggling piece and ate it without breaking eye contact. She swallowed, then wiped the corner of her mouth with her thumb. Eric found the movement mesmerizing.

"If you'd rather not take your meals with me—"

"I want to do everything with you," he insisted.

She pressed her lips together. Her tongue peeked out as she licked at the tender flesh. Eric had the urge to bite the plumpest part of her mouth. Or the corner. Anything he could sink his teeth into.

"Is a human queen always at her king's side?"

"I don't know about other men. My mother was always behind my father. I think I'd like to keep you at my side where I can see you."

"Afraid I might stab you in the back?"

"I was defenseless when you found me unconscious. I don't fear what you might do if my back was turned. There's nothing I have to hide from you."

She popped the last shrimp in her mouth and chewed. She watched him. Eric didn't break the gaze. She was testing him. He had no idea of the answer but hoped he would pass.

"If we have nothing to hide from each other, I see no reason we shouldn't marry now."

Eric blinked, thrown off balance—not by the proposal but by the absolute certainty in her tone. No hesitation. No coyness. Just fact.

"The bonds of marriage, and the vows we speak, will tie us together," she continued.

Eric leaned forward, his hand brushing the edge of hers on the table, his fingers itching to close the space between them. "I was tied to you the moment your lips touched mine and you breathed life back into me."

She uncurled her fingers and rested them in his. There were claws at the tips of them. There were gills in her neck. He only saw them because of the slight gap where skin met skin.

They were so different. But he felt like she was so completely right for him. The only person in the world for him. And he would have her.

"If you want my vows, princess, I'll gladly give them to you."

CHAPTER TEN

Once again, Ursula's hand rested lightly on Prince Eric's arm. Once again, she found herself enjoying the solid warmth of him beneath her fingers. He insisted on offering his support, as if she were dainty, as if she needed it.

She didn't. But she didn't mind. Because he felt good.

He was so solid, so strong. The muscle beneath his shirt shifted with every step. And gods, he smelled better than any man had a right to—salt and leather and sun-warmed. The scent teased her with every breath, urging her to stick out her tongue and lick.

He was so nice to look at, too. Broad shoulders, sharp jaw, that easy, confident smile set within the fertile brown of his features. She had known men who carried power, but none who wore it so effortlessly as did her prince.

Her prince? Yes, her prince. She might keep him. After she took back her crown, after she reclaimed what was rightfully hers, maybe she'd return for him. He'd be worth coming to shore for. Worth tangling her fin with.

The church loomed ahead, its stone walls weathered by salt and time. The great wooden doors stood open in welcome to all from land, sky, and sea. The scent of wax, damp stone, and distant incense drifted from within, mixing with the briny sea breeze that wound through the marketplace.

Ursula had never been inside a human place of worship. She had no use for their gods or their rituals. But power? Power was found in spoken vows, in written alliances, in the weight of words binding two people together. If Prince Eric wanted to give her that power, she would take it.

"Not sure why we're even bothering with an alliance," a passerby scoffed, loud enough for half the marketplace to hear. "Nothing good ever came from the sea, especially not from that witch."

That witch? There were plenty of witches in Evermore. The passerby could've been talking about the Snow Queen, who was a witch.

"I reckon it's the sea witch is the reason for ships sinking. She called the kraken all them years ago."

"I hear she's as ugly as an octopus, with tentacles."

Heat flared through Ursula like a spark igniting dry oil. Anger flashed hot in her veins. Her jaw tensed, ready to let out her song. She'd summon the tide, call the kraken onto dry land to drown that fool where he stood. The murmur of agreement from a few others only deepened her fury.

Eric must have felt the shift in her posture because he glanced down, his eyes narrowing at the tension in her shoulders. "The sea witch? That's your aunt?"

"Yes." The lie felt fuzzy on Ursula's tongue. So she gave him a truth. "She's not an octopus. She's a siren."

"Like you?"

Ariel was nothing like her. The child had no conception of how to use her powers. Because there had been no one to teach her after they kicked Ursula out of the kingdom.

"You care for her?" Eric continued.

"She saved me as a child. Though I didn't deserve it."

"Don't say that."

"It's true. I was an unholy brat back then."

"You grew up to be my hero. And now you'll be my bride. You wouldn't be here without her. If ever I were to come face to face with her, I would offer her my gratitude."

"You would be the only man to do so. My father—my grandfather cast her out unjustly."

"Then we will extend an olive branch for her in our kingdom," he said simply.

Ursula blinked. "What?"

"She's family, isn't she?" He squeezed her fingers lightly. "If she saved your life by calling for help against humans who meant you harm, I would consider her my ally."

It was a small thing, those words. The hand gesture. A simple acceptance, a quiet promise. But it stole the breath from Ursula's lungs.

She had spent her life knowing betrayal, knowing what it was to be silenced, to be cast aside, to be unworthy. This naïve prince with his easy trust and acceptance was lucky she was going to be here to protect him. He'd given her the shirt off his back, for Poseidon's sake.

"Are you worried?" she asked.

Eric gave a lopsided smile as he looked down at her. "Worried?"

"About my siren song." Ursula tilted her chin, watching his reaction carefully. "Do you think I'll use it against you?"

He didn't flinch. Didn't look away. Instead, he smiled, slow and knowing, as if the idea genuinely amused him. "I doubt it would have any effect on me."

Oh? So he was one of those. One of those men who thought he was different, that he could turn a woman's eye from her husband—or her girlfriend. One of those men who thought the rules didn't apply to him.

"I fell under your spell when you saved me. When you breathed life back into me. I can't think of anything you could ask of me that I wouldn't give to you."

Ursula should have felt satisfaction at that. Should have rejoiced in his gratitude, in his growing devotion. But he wasn't done.

"I'm offering you my hand in marriage. I only hope one day to win your heart."

The world around her blurred. The sounds of the marketplace dulled to a distant hum. The voices of the crowd that had irritated her were forgotten. For the first time in her life, Ursula was tongue-tied. She had no words, no clever retort, no sly quip. Nothing at all.

She had stolen a thousand voices in her time. Had taken the wills of men and women alike. But this man had just unmoored her.

She looked away from the prince. A ship rocked gently in the harbor, its sails catching the wind too perfectly, its hull just a little too polished for a vessel claiming to be a humble merchant ship. But it wasn't the ship itself that made her pulse quicken. It was the flag.

The emblem stitched into the fabric looked

innocuous enough to an untrained eye, the symbol of a distant trade guild. Ursula knew better. It was a false flag. A deception meant to mask allegiance, to slip past watchful eyes unnoticed.

A ship like that wasn't here for trade. It was here to spy, to steal, to prepare for something far more dangerous. She would know. She'd made deals with other kingdoms, sold intel, and played the double agent.

She almost pointed it out to Eric.

Almost.

The words died before they could leave her lips. She couldn't afford to be too knowledgeable, too sharp, too aware. Ariel wasn't supposed to know the markings of rival kingdoms, the tactics of war, the flags of deception. So instead, she tilted her head, forcing curiosity into her voice, and let herself become Ariel again.

"Oh," she mused, eyes wide with feigned innocence, "that's such a lovely symbol."

Eric followed her gaze, brows creasing into a flat line as he studied the flag.

"The red reminds me of corals in the reef. I think I saw something like it before," she continued, keeping her tone light, airy, offhanded. "Somewhere near the"— she hesitated as if struggling to remember, then smiled like she'd just placed it—"the capital of Ravenhold, wasn't it?"

She felt his posture shift beside her. Eric's attention

lingered on the ship for just a second longer than it should have, his lips pressing together in thought. Then he smiled at her. Easy. Carefree. As though waving it off, dismissing it as a meaningless observation.

His hand slid from hers, fingers curling subtly into a fist at his side. "Do you mind if we take a slight delay? I just want to check on a shipment."

"Of course, Your Highness."

"Eric. It's always Eric to you, Ariel."

CHAPTER ELEVEN

He wanted to kiss her.

Gods, he wanted to kiss her.

Eric stood close enough to feel the warmth of Ariel's skin, to see the seawater drying in droplets along her collarbone, to watch the delicate rise and fall of her chest as she breathed. And then a flutter at her neck—her gills.

He'd been fascinated by them since watching her eat at lunch. The differences between them—her gills, her claws, her eating habits—should've given him pause at least. Instead, he was fascinated by each and every nuance of her. Especially her mouth.

She licked her lips as she regarded him. Was that an invitation? Did he have the right to kiss her?

They were betrothed by treaty, bound by duty. They

were headed to state their vows to one another. But she hadn't asked for a kiss, and she was an innocent.

Their first kiss had been a life-giving one—and he hadn't even been conscious for it. He would be the next time. He would gorge himself on it, he was certain. It would be his second kiss.

He'd had plenty of opportunity for flings, just not a lot of time. There was always a matter of state or a crisis created by his father and the king's excesses. Eric had kept his head down and his lips pursed as he worked through problem after problem. It looked like it was going to pay off.

He literally had the woman of his dreams in his arms. The next words he'd speak to her would be vows of forever and fidelity. Then he could spend the rest of the night, the rest of his days practicing and perfecting kissing her.

So he shouldn't kiss her now. He should wait. It would only be a few more minutes.

Minutes of him aching to touch her, to press his mouth to hers and see if her kiss tasted like salt and freedom, like the memory that had haunted him since the shipwreck.

He swallowed, trying to find sense in the chaos of emotion stirring in him. Was it madness to want her this much after only moments on land?

But it wasn't only moments. He'd known her before

he'd known her name. She was the voice in the water. The red flame in the dark.

Red. There was something about red. Something important. Her voice, earlier… what had she said?

The flag. She'd pointed out the strange flag, commented offhandedly that she'd seen it in another kingdom.

Eric's head turned, the movement sharp. The ship in question still lingered in the harbor, sails slack in the salt-heavy breeze. A symbol gleamed on the mast.

Wrong ship. Wrong flag. Wrong course.

He led Ariel down the dock, guiding her aboard a naval ship with quiet assurances, murmuring to the guard to see to her comfort and keep her aboard. Only once she was seated with a cloak over her shoulders did he turn back, face set.

He crossed the harbor in long, purposeful strides and found his lieutenant near the bow of a smaller patrol cutter. The wind had shifted. Eric could feel it—the tension on the dock, the watchful stillness of his guards as they stood poised, waiting for orders. The salty breeze carried the scent of damp wood and brine, but beneath it, there was something else.

The stench of deception.

The flagged ship had been docked too perfectly, its sails furled too neatly, its crew too disciplined for a simple merchant vessel. The false flag had been meant to trick them, to lull his men into believing this was just another ship passing through his waters.

Eric wasn't fooled. "Board that ship."

Steel clanked against steel as his men moved into position, ropes thrown, swords drawn. Boots thundered against the wooden planks as they climbed aboard.

Minutes passed. Then—a cry rang out. Guards reappeared, dragging men in tattered cloaks and dull armor onto the docks. The culprits were unmasked, their faces hard with defiance.

Ravenhold.

The kingdom that had refused to sign the treaty. A shard of coastline carved from jagged cliffs and darker ambitions, Ravenhold had long nursed a bitter grudge against the Coastal Crown. Their rulers dealt in secrets and sabotage, too proud to bow to alliances, too greedy to leave the trade routes alone.

Eric's enemies had almost slipped past his defenses, had nearly succeeded in bringing their treachery into his kingdom. The guards were already praising him, voices echoing across the dock.

"A sharp eye, Your Highness."

"We would've let them pass right through."

"Brilliant work, sire."

Eric felt an urge to brush their praise aside. It hadn't been his keen awareness. He'd been too busy trying to control his desire for his bride. She had likely just saved them all with her observation.

Was it an observation? Or had she known?

She couldn't have known. Could she?

One thing he knew for certain: He wanted to kiss her. But he wanted to keep her safe even more.

Eric turned as Ariel emerged from the royal ship with guards at her side. She may have been a princess, but she strolled forward like a queen, expecting her due. His pants tightened, not uncomfortably. There was no discomfort in how much he wanted her.

"It was my bride-to-be who pointed it out," Eric told the captain as Ariel approached.

Her lips parted slightly, eyes widening just a touch. Something flickered behind them—surprise? Startlement? Maybe he had been wrong. Maybe she had only made a passing remark about the pretty flag.

The guards and naval officers, one by one, turned to face her. Their hardened expressions shifted. Bows were offered—some stiff with discipline, others more reverent. One man even thumped a fist to his chest.

"Your Highness," the captain said with a respectful incline of his head toward her. "We owe you our thanks."

That was definitely surprise on her face. But it was the kind of surprise Eric had seen while moving chess pieces across a board. It was the surprise when his opponent uncovered the sneak attack he'd been planning since the first move.

Ariel dipped her chin in a gracious nod, her expression smoothing into something demure.

Eric watched her closely. There was pride in her bearing, but not the kind born from flattery. It was older, deeper, like a queen remembering how to wear a crown.

The ship's captain stepped forward. "Your Highness, it would be my honor to escort you and the future queen back to the castle. There's concern for your safety after today's events."

Eric shook his head. "Thank you, but we've an errand to run first. One that will last into the night."

CHAPTER TWELVE

Ursula could taste victory on the tip of her tongue. Just a few more steps. Just a few more words spoken, and everything she had lost would be hers again.

Eric's vows would seal it. His pledge, his name, his title—they would all become hers. She inhaled through her mouth, and then again through her gills, pulling the moisture out of the air, double savoring of victory.

She had outwitted her brother, slipped past his defenses like the tide creeping over land. She had won. She almost pumped her fist in triumph, ready to relish the moment—except something stopped her.

Something warm. Solid. Steady.

Eric was still holding her hand. Not just holding it

with his palm pressed to hers. No, his fingers were entwined with hers, down to the webbing of her digits.

She would have expected his hands to be soft, the hands of a pampered prince who let others do the work. But they weren't. There were calluses along his palms, rough edges along his fingertips—marks of a man who touched the world instead of merely ruling over it.

In the last few hours that she'd known the prince, he'd shown himself to be the kind of man who stepped forward instead of standing back. The kind of man who threw himself into the fire, into the water, into the battle—not for glory but because he couldn't stand to let others burn. A man who earned respect instead of demanding it.

He was likely going to get himself killed one day. Men like him—leaders who rushed into battle at the front instead of standing behind the grunts— always did.

He squeezed her fingers again, infusing his warmth into her. Those hands could easily pick her up, carry her, cradle her while she rested. The fool man would ensure her safety, not letting any harm come to her as he pressed her to his chest. She would have to make sure to hold him back, keep him in line when she commanded his army to attack her brother and the Sea Kingdom.

"You don't have to do this." His voice was a quiet rumble against her temple. "I'll protect you from your father whether we're married or not."

Her father was long dead and returned to the seabed. Oh, right. Eric didn't mean her father. He meant Ariel's.

"My kingdom may not be as vast as the sea, but anything that is mine"—he brought their clasped hands to his chest, over his heart—"will be yours."

No conditions. No obligations. Just a promise. Yes, this man definitely needed a woman like her in his life to protect him.

"Because I saved your life?" Ursula asked.

Eric's fingers traced her cheek and slid down to her jaw. When his thumb brushed over her lower lip, a shudder rolled through her. "Because you made my life worth living."

Ursula stopped breathing. She had two ways to pull oxygen into her lungs. Both failed her.

"I want to spend my life with you. But I'll never force you to do something you don't want to do."

"You are forcing me to do something." She tipped her face up to his, watching as his pupils dilated. Dragging her hands up his chest, she felt the rapid thrum of his heartbeat beneath her fingertips. "You're forcing me to wait longer than necessary to claim my husband."

His sharp inhale, the way his grip on her waist tightened, sent a thrill curling down her spine. "I'm yours to command, my siren."

Ursula didn't care to tell him what to do. She was far more interested in watching what he came up with. Because everything he'd done since she'd pulled him out of the sea had been aimed at her. It was the best foreplay of her life.

The air inside the temple was thick with incense and the sharp scent of sea salt, the kind that lingered on the skin, in the hair, long after one had left the water. Candles flickered in the carved alcoves of the stone walls, casting shadows that danced like rippling waves. At the center of it all stood the mage. Her hair was as white as sea foam, long and straight. Her face was unlined, timeless, as if she had stepped through the ages without them touching her. She regarded them with steady, piercing eyes—the color of pearls beneath the moonlight.

Ursula had met enough mages in her time to know that the most powerful ones never showed their true age. Still, she lifted her chin and held the woman's gaze, daring her to question why she, the long-lost princess of the sea, was standing beside the Coastal prince, hand in hand.

"We want to be married today," Eric announced.

The mage's lips twitched. "The wedding was set for next tide."

"That will be the state ceremony, for the court, for politics, for treaties and kingdoms. But this…" Eric's thumb stroked absently over the back of Ursula's hand. "This will be just for us."

The mage tilted her head, considering them both. "Why so eager, Your Highness?"

"Blame my racing heart," Eric said with a charming grin that Ursula had no doubt got him his way without his crown.

The mage's gaze flicked to Ursula. For a single, tense-filled moment, it felt as though the ageless woman saw everything.

The truth.

The deception.

The game Ursula was playing.

The mage inhaled slowly, drawing in the air like she was listening to something beyond their ears. "Perhaps your heart is racing because it hears a lulling song."

Ursula went still. Her pulse slammed against her ribs, her stomach twisting into a cold knot. *She knows. She knows, she knows, she knows—*

"You are not the expected tune," the mage mused, her fingers curling as if plucking invisible threads of fate. "But I think the two of you together will make a great song for all peoples."

Beside Ursula, Eric smiled, looking as if he could hear the music the mage predicted they would make.

The mage reached forward, taking their joined hands, her grip cool but steady. And as the ritual began, Ursula thought of all the things she would gain from this union: her throne, her vengeance, her rightful place in the sea.

As the mage spoke the first words of binding, Eric's grip on her hand tightened. It wasn't painful. It wasn't possessive.

No, that wasn't quite true. There was a claim in it—a quiet, steady assertion that she belonged to him. What startled Ursula was how little she minded the claim.

The mage's voice echoed through the temple. It was laced with an ancient magic that hummed in the air like a melody woven through time. The glow of candlelight flickered against the carved stone walls, illuminating the symbols of land, sea, and sky—a reminder that this world was vast, made of more than just one kingdom, one people, one way of being.

"We gather here beneath sky and stone, before the watchful eyes of those who came before us to weave together two fates, two lives, two souls—so that from this day forward, no tide nor storm, no claw nor blade, no force of nature nor magic nor time itself shall pull them apart."

There was power in vows. Power greater than gems or spells or even the rule of kings.

"Prince Eric of the Western Shores, son of the

House of Tiberian, heir to the throne of men—do you stand before us freely? Willingly? With a heart unburdened and a soul unchained?"

"I do."

"Ariel of—"

"No," Ursula insisted. "Call me by my true name: Siren."

"Siren of the Abyssal Depths, daughter of the Sea King's bloodline, heir to the tides—do you stand before us freely? Willingly? With a heart unburdened and a soul unchained?"

"I do," Ursula said, the words rolling off her tongue like the touch of silk on her damp flesh. It tried to glide, but in some spots it clung.

The mage lifted her arms. The magic in the air thickened, wrapping around them in unseen threads, binding them together in ways that no paper contract, no royal decree, no crown could undo.

"Then speak your vows."

Eric turned to her, his dark eyes full and eager. "I vow to walk beside you. Where you lead, I will follow. Where you stand, I will stand. I vow to protect you. I vow to see you and to know you as I know myself because from this day, we are one."

Ursula licked her lips, and for once, she didn't craft a lie, didn't shape her words to deceive. "I vow to walk beside you. Where you lead, I will follow. Where you stand, I will stand. I vow to protect you. I vow to see you and to know you as I know myself because from this day, we are one."

The mage placed her hands over theirs. "Then by the laws of the land, the tides, the sky, and all who bear witness this day, you are bound. You may seal your vows with a kiss."

CHAPTER THIRTEEN

Eric couldn't stop touching her. Not after their vows had been spoken, not after the magic bound them in ways that no kingdom, no war, no decree could undo. His hands found her waist, her hips, the small of her back, pulling her close as he kissed her, his lips urgent, desperate, wanting.

His wife.

The words thrummed through him, his pulse beating in time with the song the mage accused his heart of playing. It was her song—his siren's song.

She melted into him, fingers curling into his shirt. Her breath was warm against his cheek. Her body molded to his as if she had always belonged there.

They'd made it out of the temple, but he knew for a certainty they would not make it back to the castle. He didn't want to go back to the castle. Because the moment they crossed its manicured gardens, responsibility would come crashing down on him again—the treaties, the politics, the weight of his father's legacy and his pressing against his shoulders.

But here, on the docks, with her? There was nothing but the sea breeze, the taste of salt on her lips, the way she looked at him like he was hers just as much as she was his. This he wanted to do forever.

Eric broke the kiss, breathless, and took her hand. "Come with me."

She didn't hesitate. She trusted him. Completely. It made his heart thump in his chest, another wild, flipping beat of the organ, as he led her down a pier.

Waters lapped against the wooden beams. Waves rocked the ships moored to their posts. Lanterns cast golden pools of light along the pier, swaying in the breeze.

Eric led her to a houseboat nestled near the end of the dock, smaller than the royal fleet but sturdy, well-kept, the wood dark and polished by years of sea air. The sails were furled neatly. The deck was cluttered with ropes and barrels. A small lantern hung from a post, glowing softly against the setting sun.

"This was the first boat I learned to sail on," he told her, running a hand over the railing. "The first time I took her out alone, I thought I was going to capsize. The sea knocked me around like a rag doll."

"I bet you loved it."

"Always have. If I hadn't been born a prince… I would've been a sailor."

"It's no wonder you married a fish."

Eric laughed, the sound bright and free. But then… his laughter faded. Something else settled into his chest. Her words were a joke, but they were also the truth.

He had just married a siren. A woman born of the sea. A creature with magic in her veins and gills at her neck. In the water, she had a tail. On land she had feet. But… what about the rest of her anatomy?

Eric hesitated, trying to find the proper words. Words that would inform and not offend. Yet every way he could possibly phrase it sounded ridiculous, offensive, or like something out of an old sailor's bawdy bar song.

Ariel tilted her head, watching him. "You look like you're about to walk off the plank."

"I just—" He ran a hand over the back of his neck. "I'm just wondering… Are we… compatible?"

For a moment, she just stared at him. It was clear the way her blue eyes dimmed then brightened that she puzzled out his meaning. Then she burst out laughing. It was a full, unrestrained sound, rich and warm, her head tipping back as it rang across the dock.

"I mean—" Eric scrubbed a hand down his face, half-exasperated, half-relieved. "It's a valid question."

"Oh, my sweet prince," she purred, stepping closer, pressing a hand to his chest, fingers curling over his heartbeat. "You're in for a very, very pleasant surprise."

She pulled him aboard. Like he'd said in his vows, Eric followed. Once they were within the shelter of the cabin and away from prying eyes, she tugged at the ties of her gown. The fabric fell down her body like a waterfall, coming to pool at her feet.

Back on the beach, Eric had tried not to look. Tried and failed. Now his gaze dipped to the V between her thighs. He'd expected a red thatch of curls, like the hair on her head. She was hairless. Her flesh glistened there, as though she was ready for him.

"We'll go slowly," he promised.

"You've had me waiting around all day. Either you take me now or I'm going to jump your bones."

"It'll hurt your first time if we don't go slowly."

"It's not my—that's not my concern. It shouldn't be your concern, either."

"Your comfort, your pleasure, your happiness—those will always be my first concerns."

She smiled at him. The smile started as a thing of amusement. Before his eyes, it melted into something tender.

"I'm excited to do this together," he said, cupping her cheek. "It will be one of our many firsts."

"Our firsts?"

He nodded. "I waited for you."

"You… did?"

"Mainly because I was too busy with duties to even consider a lover. Now I have absolutely no desire to go back to my duties. I have a feeling I'm going to want to spend every waking moment being naked with you."

"Well, then, you're behind on that front. You are far too dressed."

He stepped back from her, less than an arm's length. He didn't want to spend another day, another moment with his wife farther away than he could reach. With his own hands, he began peeling his clothes off. "Don't be frightened."

"Fear is the last thing I'm feeling right now."

He believed her. Her eyes roamed over his body with hungry glances. When he pulled off his breeches, a smile split her face.

"Thank the stars you're not a guppy." And with that statement, she reached for him.

"Ariel don't-ahh!" His bride held his manhood in a vise. Not a painful one. Not a fearful one either.

"Siren," she corrected him with a squeeze of his cock. "Either you let me have a taste or I'll sing to you and have you dancing to my tune. Regardless of which you choose, I'm going to have my way with you."

Eric grinned his pleasure. He'd been concerned about this moment, their wedding night. Worrying it would be awkward and tear-filled. Once again, his new wife surprised him.

"Sing to me," he commanded.

"No." Both her voice and her hands stroked at him. "I'd rather have you sing to me."

By the second stroke, Eric was singing her tune. She sank to her knees and added her tongue to the symphony of sensations. Eric hit a high note when she swallowed him whole and hummed around his length. He had no idea where she'd learned to do this. He didn't want to think about it. It was too good. He was going to reach his climax if she didn't—

She came off him with a pop before he was unmanned. "I want to feel you inside of me."

Eric had no more arguing in him. He was dancing to her tune, and she hadn't sung a note. It had been his groans of pleasure filling the cabin. Now he wanted to hear her moan.

She reached for the seashell bra still cover her breasts and unclasped the garment. Red-peaked nipples stared back at him, causing his mouth to water more.

His bride slid back onto the mattress. Eric followed, prowling up her lithe body. Though she was made of curves, he still dwarfed her with his size. By the look of it, she was reveling in it.

He'd meant those vows of protection. He hadn't missed the flare of her nostrils as he'd said those particular words back at the temple. She wanted his protection. She would have it for the rest of his days. But first, he needed to claim her.

He lined himself up with her entrance. Despite what she'd told him, he was going to take this slowly. He pushed into her core, just a little. She made a delighted sound that turned to frustration when he didn't push all the way in.

She flashed those blue eyes at him in warning. Eric withdrew.

She bared her sharp teeth at him. Eric grinned and pushed in a little more.

Again, he got a sigh, followed by a groan of irritation. Oh, how he was going to love their fights as well as their make-ups. He was happily thinking about how he was going to torture his wife when his brain turned off the logical parts and his pleasure sensors took over. He had tried to resist the soft, velvety feel of her. What a foolish errand.

Her slickness urged him deeper. Her intimate muscles pulled him farther inside. There was no barrier as he pushed deeper.

Did sirens not have a maidenhead? It was as though

she'd done this before. As though they'd done this before. As though they were made for each other.

Eric tried to slow down, tried to be gentle. Neither his body nor her body were hearing of it. He sank into her like an anchor dropping into the water. The tide pulled them together. Eric plunged until he bottomed out.

And that's when he heard his siren sing. It was accompanied by his baritone roar.

CHAPTER FOURTEEN

Ursula lay tangled in the sheets, her body humming from the pleasures Eric had given her. For a novice, the man was good—damn good. He'd stroked her in places the eels had never reached. His arms stayed wrapped around her long after the last shuddering gasp of release, holding her close like she was precious—or as if he thought she might disappear if he let go.

She should have wanted to go. She never lingered. Never craved a male's warmth. Yet here she was, curled against her prince, her palm resting over his steady heartbeat. Her body thrumming with the memory of how he had worshiped her.

It was absurd that this man, this prince, had been a virgin. She had expected clumsy eagerness, rushed fumbling, blind hunger. Instead, she had gotten devotion, restraint, patience that bordered on reverence—for the second time.

The first time had been desperate, quick, overwhelming. But still good. Great, even.

The second time had been slower, deeper, like he was learning her—memorizing every sound she made, every place on her body that made her arch, made her tremble. By the third time, he wasn't just touching her. He was ruining her.

Prince Eric acted as if he had all the time in the world on their wedding night. He'd used his patience, dragging pleasure out of her until her body was boneless, pliant. Until she had forgotten everything but the feel of him inside her, over her, surrounding her.

Ursula shifted, stretching. The ache that rippled through her wasn't just from what they'd done in the sheets. She had been on land too long. Her lungs could manage the air, but her gills needed water. A full, deep breath of the sea, something cold and unfiltered.

She slipped carefully from Eric's arms. He murmured something in his sleep, his grip tightening before he exhaled and relaxed back into the pillows. She let herself linger long enough to take in the sight of him—bare, sprawled out in tangled sheets. His skin kissed by moonlight. His dark curls tousled from her fingers, raking through them.

Then she slipped out of the cabin, off the boat, and into the sea.

The moment the water touched her skin, the magic surged through her. Her legs fused, flesh rippling like liquid silver. Her knees bent and reformed. Her feet flattened into the smooth, sleek fin of her tail. The sensation was more liberation than pain.

Her skin shimmered in the moonlit water, bioluminescent lines along her tail pulsing. Her gills opened to drink in deep, sweet lungfuls of salt and current and life. She flipped once, then again, spiraling through the water like a creature unshackled, muscles stretching in ways they had been aching to.

This was who she was. Not a woman in silks and jewels. Not a bride standing at an altar. Not a body tangled in a prince's sheets.

She was of the sea. She belonged to the depths. When she surfaced, brushing her hair back, she saw him.

Eric stood at the edge of the boat, watching her. His arms were braced against the railing, the same arms that had been wrapped around her not moments before. His hair was mussed from her passionate caresses, his bare chest bathed in moonlight. He was gloriously naked and unashamed.

"May I join you?"

He waited patiently for her answer. He didn't take

for granted that his place beside her was his due as her husband. He didn't assume that it was his right as a prince. It was clear by his erection that he wanted her again, but he was waiting for her consent.

Ursula gave it.

His body broke the water, and she swore the temperature of the water rose a few degrees. Eric moved like he was born of the tide, slicing through the dark waves with effortless grace. His strong shoulders flexed as he swam toward her. Not like a man who had just woken from tangled sheets, warm and sated from their bedsport. Not like a prince weighted by duty and expectation. Like someone unburdened, weightless, free.

When he reached her, he did not speak. He simply looked at her. His gaze tracked the slope of her bare shoulders, the soft swell of her un-shelled breasts, the way her flesh tapered into shimmering scales, leading down to the powerful sweep of her iridescent tail.

There was no fear in his expression. No unease. No hesitation. Only wonder.

"You're beautiful."

Ursula's fin flicked involuntarily beneath the water, sending tiny ripples over the surface. She had been admired before, worshiped before. So why did this feel different?

"I needed to stretch my fin. And take a breath of the

sea." She reached up, brushing her hair away from the side of her neck, exposing the slits of her gills. "Just as you can hold your breath beneath the waves, I can do the same on land. But eventually, I have to return to the sea."

Eric's hand lifted slowly, hesitantly, fingers hovering just inches away from the delicate ridges of her gills.

He wasn't assuming.

He wasn't taking.

He was asking.

Ursula tilted her head, offering him her throat. His fingers brushed against the sensitive skin. It was barely more than a whisper of contact. A shudder rolled through her, down the length of her spine, all the way to the tips of her fin.

The prince watched her reaction. Fascination lit his face. Delight tugged at the corner of his mouth. With agonizing slowness, he leaned in. His breath fanned warm against her skin, a contrast to the cool water surrounding them. And then—

His lips pressed to her gills. A sharp, pleasure-laced moan tore from Ursula's throat before she could stop it. Eric's lips dragged over the sensitive ridges. His hand slid to the curve of her waist, steadying her as another shiver wracked her body. Ursula gripped his shoulders, claws digging in.

"You like that?" he asked.

She growled, her tail flicking around him, pulling his body closer to her own.

Eric dipped his head again, pressing another kiss to her gills. He ran his tongue over the flesh, the tip lingering. Then his lips closed around her gills, and he sucked. Ursula let out a gurgled moan and sank into the waters, pulling him down with her.

The current caught them, spinning them weightless beneath the waves. Ursula barely noticed. Because his hands were on her, gripping her waist as he pulled her flush against him, his mouth hot despite the cool water, his kiss deep and searching and desperate.

The sea wrapped around them, but Eric didn't pull away. Didn't surface. Didn't seem to realize he was running out of air.

Ursula realized it for him. She felt it in the tension in his body, in the way his fingers tightened against her skin, in the flutter of his pulse beneath her palms. She slid her hands into his hair, holding him firmly against her gills. His body relaxed as she exhaled into him, her gills flexing, releasing a cool rush of oxygen-rich air.

Eric breathed her in, then licked the raised skin again and again. Inhale, suckle. Inhale, suckle. It was the most erotic thing Ursula had ever experienced in her life.

Just like when he was inside her body, he kissed her like he had all the time in the world. Like the sea couldn't pull him away. Then, just when she thought she might lose herself completely, he pulled away—not to surface, not to panic, not to gasp for air. But to press his mouth back to hers.

He kissed her lips deeply. He kissed her mouth hungrily. He kissed her like he would never stop.

Ursula was glad she had saved his life. She patted herself on the back for her brilliant idea of impersonating her niece and snagging this man. And she was definitely going to keep this prince of the coast after she took back the sea.

CHAPTER FIFTEEN

The first blush of dawn painted the horizon in soft hues of rose and gold, casting its light through the curtained window of the houseboat. The gentle sway of the water rocked them, a rhythm so steady, so soothing, that Eric almost forgot the weight of the world waiting for him beyond these walls.

Almost.

His fingers trailed along Ariel's back, tracing the elegant dip of her spine. Her skin was soft, warm. He could still remember the feel of her scales when she had a fin instead of legs. She'd been soft and warm then, too. But different.

She was different. Different from any woman he'd ever met. Not that he had paid much attention to the women in the court trying to catch his eye. He'd always known his would be a diplomatic marriage, like his parents and his grandparents before him. He'd never imagined that love would be in the cards for him. But here he was, falling, drowning in his emotions.

It was impossible to forget the way her gills had given him breath. How her body had sustained his under water. How she had pressed her lips to his in the depths and made the sea feel like home.

Only yesterday, he had resented this marriage. Resented the chains it had placed on him, the powerlessness of being forced into a treaty forged by their fathers.

But now—

Now as his wife lay entangled with him, he knew he would wage a war against anyone who asked him to move even an inch. Her steady breaths tickled against his bare chest, but laughter was far from his mind.

He felt thankful. So thankful. So at peace. With himself. With the world. With… everything. He couldn't imagine another moment, another day, another life without her in it. That's when a sharp surge of anger sliced through him.

What if it hadn't worked?

What if Triton had tossed his daughter into the arms of some other man, treating her like a bargaining chip instead of a woman with her own mind, her own desires?

His wife was a treasure. A bright light that had already made his life better. And all of it outside any of the parameters of the treaty between their kingdoms.

The treaty hadn't solved anything. It was built on threats, on desperation, not trust. Humans still did not have safe passage through the seas. Pirates and hunters still trafficked in black market gems and sunken goods. The balance hadn't shifted. Except for one thing.

Eric loved his wife. It had barely been a day, but he knew this fact like he knew his soul. He loved Ariel fiercely, wholly, with a protectiveness that bordered on something primal. And he would never let anything, anyone, harm her.

His siren let out a soft inhale as she began to wake, her body shifting against his beneath the sheets. Eric dipped his head, pressing his lips to her gills. He let his mouth linger there, where her breath had once sustained his own.

Her body tensed, then relaxed, her fingers curling against his chest. He moved his mouth up, brushing his lips to her temple. Then down to her cheek. And finally, against her mouth. When her eyes fluttered open, he kissed her again. Deeper this time, as if he could pour all the unspoken vows he still hadn't said into her skin.

When he pulled back, he pressed his forehead to hers, his voice a low vow against her lips. "I'm going to fix this."

"What did you break, my prince?"

"I didn't break anything. Neither of us did. It was our fathers and their decades-old distrust of each other."

She pulled away from him. That's when he remembered that she had been a victim in the senseless war between their kind.

"I know that you were targeted by hunters as a child. I thank the sands that you were unharmed."

"You should thank Ursula for that."

"If she were here, I would."

That appeared to mollify his siren.

"The problem with the treaty is it's based on threats," he continued. "It needs to be an alliance, one like we have. One where we come together and bring out the best in each other."

"You think you bring out the best in me?"

"I know you bring out the best in me. In just one day, I'm a better man, a better leader because of you. You're going to make me an exceptional king."

She cocked her head, studying him. "Yes, I believe I will."

"We need to demand safe passage across all of the sea from Triton."

"You went quickly from exceptional to demanding. Triton doesn't control the sea monsters. They rise when men disturb them. Sailors need to stick to the prescribed routes if they want their bounty and their bodies to remain safe."

"That's doable. But I can't control pirates or hunters."

"Don't bother trying. Their lives will be forfeit if they go those routes. What you can control is the littering and destruction that goes on by sailors and seagoers. Merkind don't come to the surface and litter in your yards."

"Fair point. Anything else, my queen?"

Her head jerked in that way that Eric was coming to realize meant she hadn't been expected to be taken seriously. She had to know he would always take every word she uttered with care and consideration.

She bit at her lower lip before saying more. Eric almost missed it. All he could think about was biting that lip.

When she released hold of her lip, she said, "I want the family jewels."

"You've had your way with my family jewels all night, my love."

"Not yours. I want my family jewels returned to me from my—from Triton. He took them from me as a punishment when he felt I… misbehaved. But it was because he didn't listen to me, and I was right."

"I won't ever make that mistake. I will always listen to you. And I'll get you your jewels."

"Then we have a deal."

Eric held out his hand in the same way he'd seal a political or economic deal. After a flash of a grin, Ariel took his hand. When her fingers met his, he pulled her to him. She gasped into his kiss.

"I expected you to be more demure, princess," he said when he came up for air. Instead of breathing the sea air, Eric pressed his mouth to her gills. That rare air was quickly becoming his favorite taste.

"I've been silent too long. And now I'm a queen."

"You never have to hold your tongue with me."

"You very much like what I do with my tongue."

"You're right. Especially when you sing for me. When I move inside of you. When I kiss your lips or your gills. Those are my favorite songs. I'll have you sing them every day, sing until you're hoarse."

Her expression was somber, serious. "They're your songs, my prince. Only for you."

"Only for me." Eric pressed his lips to her neck again, licking over her gills, up the column of her neck, and to the edge of her lips. "Sing for me now, siren."

He felt his wife's intake of breath in preparation for a song. Before she could get out the first note, there was a knock at the door.

CHAPTER SIXTEEN

The carriage rocked gently as it rolled down the road. The rhythmic clatter of hooves against cobblestone filled the silence that stretched thick and tense between them.

Not the tension between Ursula and Eric.

They sat close—too close for comfort, too far for satisfaction. His hand was still wrapped around hers from when they'd reluctantly left the boathouse. Those hands had dressed her. He'd fastened the clamshells over her breast. He'd refastened the sapphire gem around her neck. He'd pulled the silk gown over her limbs. The fabric had slid down her heated flesh like a twilight wave—smooth, cool, and sinful. It clung to her curves, molded to every line of her body, hiding nothing from the man who'd just vowed his life to her.

His eyes had followed the descent of the silk like it was a ceremony unto itself, his touch lingering longer than necessary.

Now their fingers twined together like seaweed and netting. Her prince hadn't let go. Neither had she.

Eric's thumb traced slow, aching circles on the back of Ursula's hand. His thigh brushed hers with every jostle of the road. The contact sent sparks up her spine. The hum of his attention was sunlight on her skin, like rays warming sea glass.

He glanced at her mouth, a slow drag of his eyes over her lips like he was hungry. Ursula curled her bottom lip between her teeth, and Eric's breath hitched. He bit his own lip in response, his gaze darkening as if the memory of their kisses last night had sunk hooks deep into him.

Ursula's free hand rested on her thigh. What would happen if she slid her hand just slightly toward his? If she leaned forward. If she claimed his mouth again.

"Fighting has broken out in Prince Phillip's kingdom."

The sexual tension between Ursula and Eric snapped. What was left was the thick miasma coming from the other side of the carriage where Grimsby sat looking down at documents, his spyglasses sitting at the edge of his long, patrician nose.

Eric exhaled sharply, his posture straightening, but

he didn't let go of Ursula's hand. "We dealt with the troll situation. How could they have gotten that far inland?"

The Inland Kingdom had been under siege by trolls for the past three years. Trolls were ugly, persistent creatures that boiled down from the mountains like a plague. The war had dragged on long enough to delay Prince Phillip's marriage to Princess Aurora, a dainty but powerful heiress of a smaller coastal realm—one whose alliance had been crucial to the treaty between the land and the sea.

"Reports are still unclear, but it's confirmed that forces breached the borders near the Eastern edge of the forest."

With his other hand, Eric rubbed at the bottom lip that Ursula had wanted to bite just seconds ago. She still wanted to bite it now. Possibly even more so.

He turned slightly from her, giving her his profile. He looked older when duty returned to his face. Sharper. Wearier. Handsome in a different way.

"The reports also say that these were not trolls attacking Prince Phillip's castle but mermen." Grimsby's gaze flicked to Ursula, acknowledging her for the first time since she'd gotten into the carriage. "The castle is said to be flooded, a tsunami-like wave overtaking the northern walls."

"A tsunami? They're too far inland for that kind of

storm. Unless…" Eric's hand tightened around hers. "A power like that could only come from the sea king."

"Or his daughter," said Grimsby.

"It's clearly not Ariel." Eric dismissed the older man. "My wife has been with me all night. You and Princess Aurora developed a friendship, I was told."

All this time Ursula thought her cover would be blown by that side-walking crab. But no, it would be unveiled by the sea princess' tantrum. What had Ariel done now?

Ursula gave Eric her most prim look. Her husband quirked a brow as though she'd just shared a joke between them.

Grimsby still looked at her with suspicion, even as his words were directed at Eric. "You think it's King Triton then? For what reason?"

"No, I don't think it's Triton." Eric toyed with a lock of her hair absently. "It must be Ursula."

Ursula stiffened.

"It's the only other logical explanation. But why would your aunt do this?"

Ursula had to fight to contain her ire. What could she say? She couldn't clear her name and say she didn't do it because she was, indeed, with him all night. Or maybe she should?

Maybe now was the time to come clean and tell Eric that she was Ursula. It wasn't like he could divorce her.

But he certainly wouldn't look at her like he was now, like she could do no wrong. Like they shared jokes between them. Like he wanted to know what she thought and would take her advice to heart.

"Is Prince Phillip unharmed?" Ursula asked instead.

"It would seem he's been taken in by the Forest Folk," said Grimsby. "He and the Forest Guardian have a… history."

Ursula knew that history well. She was willing to bet the Forest Guardian and the prince had more than a history. They had a future together. One that didn't include Phillip's intended bride. So why had Ariel razed the castle if Phillip no longer wanted to marry Aurora?

"And Princess Aurora?" Ursula asked. "Is she accounted for?"

"It would appear she's disappeared with the siren," said Grimsby. "Likely a hostage."

Ursula kept her snort in. Aurora was a hostage, all right. A willing hostage. Hopefully, she and Ariel would both stay gone.

"We should send aid to help rebuild the castle and offer to take in displaced refugees," Ursula said.

Grimsby raised a brow at the command.

"Do as your queen tells you," said Eric.

Grimsby's mouth pinched, but he nodded. "Yes, Your Majesty."

That's right. Eric was now a king, and she was his

queen. The Coastal crown had only been waiting for its prince to take a bride before the honorific and the duty passed on to him.

The carriage rocked to a stop. The moment the door swung open, sunlight flooded in, too bright, too harsh. Ursula blinked against it as Grimsby stepped out first, his posture stiff, formal, ever the perfect chamberlain.

Eric followed, his broad frame cutting a striking figure against the morning light. He turned back toward her, extending his hand. When her fingers touched his palm, the sunlight softened, appearing to coalesce around him. Only him.

The moisture in the air was clean here at the castle, waves and sunlight mixing at this elevation to satisfy both her lungs and her gills. Her legs ached from use—from last night as they had wrapped around her husband, as well as the long use of the two limbs in favor of her fin. She had to endure it just a while longer before she could unfurl herself in a tub of warm salt water.

Servants lined the grand courtyard. Courtiers stood just beyond them, watching, waiting, whispering. A sea of eyes raked over her, assessing, calculating.

Ursula reached up, trying to smooth her hair, fix the folds of her gown. She looked like she'd taken a roll in a reef. Because she had. As she looked around, she saw some uptilted smirks, some lowered brows, and some wide eyes full of wonder.

She leaned toward Eric, lowering her voice. "You didn't tell me we'd have an audience. I look like a drowned jellyfish washed up on shore."

"You look like a bride who was well loved by her husband on her wedding night."

He was right about that. She had been well loved. That was the only word to call what Prince Eric of the Coastlands had done to her body last night. He hadn't used her. He hadn't abused her. He had loved her.

Eric pressed a loving kiss to her lips now. Right there at the gates to his kingdom, where all eyes could see. When he pulled back, he smiled down at her, like a clam showing off the pearl in its belly.

"You're a rare gem, King Eric."

"I'm your rare gem, my queen."

"That you are. All mine. And I am your queen." Ursula exhaled slowly, straightened her spine, and pulled the regal air she'd been born with around herself like armor.

She had fought for this moment. For this crown, for this title. She was Queen of the Coasts. Not Queen of the Sea, not yet. But she was a queen, nonetheless.

CHAPTER SEVENTEEN

The throne room was suffocating. The heavy stone walls, the banners overhead, the long mahogany table where his council argued endlessly—it all pressed down on Eric like the hull of a sinking ship, cracking plank by plank, flooding faster than he could bail. Duty and expectation rose around him like seawater, threatening to drag him under before he could catch a breath.

For one blessed day, he had been free. For one night, he had belonged to himself, to her, to the dream they had spun between tangled sheets and whispered promises. And now?

Now his father's council bickered over whether they should send troops to Phillip's kingdom or wait for more reports. The merchants demanded tax adjustments while the navy wanted more ships to protect the trade routes. The high priest insisted upon a second, official state wedding, warning that without the gods' blessing, Eric and Ariel's rushed union could bring misfortune upon the realm.

The head of the merchant's guild complained of dwindling fish stocks, blaming Triton's restrictions on deep-sea fishing for driving up market prices. Meanwhile, a group of nobles demanded harsher penalties on black-market traders, insisting that the trafficking of sea creatures for spell components and rare delicacies was a stain on the kingdom's reputation.

And then there was the growing unease over Triton's silence. Not a word, not a messenger, not even a ripple of acknowledgment had come from the sea king since Ariel had arrived. Eric and Ariel had only been back a couple of hours, but that was long enough for a message to be delivered to and received by the Sea King.

Was he waiting? Plotting? Or simply stewing?

The weight of all of it pressed down on Eric, the demands stacking higher and higher until it felt as though the very walls of the throne room were closing in. Eric dragged a hand down his face, his patience thinning. Then the door at the far end of the hall opened, and she walked in.

His wife stood framed in the doorway, bathed in the

golden light spilling in from the corridor beyond. She wore a gown of silk so light it clung to her curves, the fabric shifting like liquid moonlight over her body. Her red hair was pinned up, revealing the graceful column of her throat, her swan-like neck leading down to the delicate curve of her shoulders.

Eric felt his body move before he could think. His hands pressed against the armrests as he rose, as if pulled toward her by an unseen force. The closer he got to her, the more the tension eased from his chest. The heaviness of his burdens lessened with every step she took toward him.

She moved like a current cutting through still water. He knew the secrets that silk gown barely hid. Each ripple made his mouth water. The late afternoon sunlight kissed the bare skin of her collarbone, glinting off the soft curve of her shoulder where the fabric slid just enough to make him want to pull it down farther. Her eyes were bright and knowing, burning with the same desire that coiled low in his stomach.

She stopped just before him, and before he could think better of it, his fingers were already reaching for hers, twining together, his thumb brushing over her pulse point, feeling it quick and strong beneath his touch. He barely heard the awkward throat-clearing of Grimsby until the man spoke.

"My queen, the ladies are meeting in the next room, sipping their tea."

"Good for them. I heard this is where the council was meeting to discuss the kingdom's business."

A beat of silence.

Grimsby blinked. Once. Twice. Clearly flustered.

"I apologize for being late," his queen continued. "I had to find a dress to my liking. My closet was filled with cotton, which is an unnatural fiber to any creature that lives in the water. Silk is much more to my liking."

Eric made a mental note to bring more silks to the castle for his wife—sea silks, river silks, moon-touched silks imported from the Frost Kingdom. Every texture. Every color. Deep-sea blue to match her eyes, storm-gray like the ocean before a tempest, and red—red like the sunlit tips of her hair as it fanned across their shared pillow.

As if he didn't already have enough responsibilities balancing treaties, training soldiers, and untangling the ever-knotting snarl of trade, now he was making space in his mind for hem lengths and fabric weights. For stitching and seams. For her.

"I thought the sea princess didn't speak." The whisper rustled through the chamber.

"Your queen heard you speaking of merchant unrest, overfishing, and the black market." Ariel's gaze tracked the voice and spoke directly to the man. "There's a simple solution to all three."

Every pair of eyes turned to her, some with barely concealed skepticism, others with thinly veiled curiosity. Eric remained silent, waiting, because he knew what they didn't.

"The issue with overfishing is where the fish are being caught. Right now, you have merchants fighting over dwindling waters because they're all restricted to one area. Meanwhile, there are entire stretches of the sea teeming with fish, untouched, simply because the routes aren't safe. If you had Triton enforce safe zones while also working with the navy to patrol those routes, you could—"

"That won't work," Lord Withersby blustered, cutting her off before she could finish. He waved a dismissive hand, as though brushing her suggestion from the room.

Eric traced gentle circles over his wife's knuckles. "What exactly makes you think it won't work, Lord Withersby?"

The old man shifted in his seat, clearly unprepared to be questioned so directly. "The merfolk would never agree to such terms, and the cost of more naval patrols would be untenable. It's... impractical. The sea folk have always been fickle."

"What if," Eric mused, still tracing the light circles across his wife's skin, "instead of restricting merchants to the same waters, we create designated safe fishing zones, monitored jointly by Triton's kingdom and our own. That way, fish populations remain stable, the merchants don't starve, and we work toward better relations with the Sea Kingdom instead of tensions escalating."

Lord Withersby perked up, stroking his beard. "Now that is an idea with merit."

Beside him, Ariel went still. Eric didn't need to look at her to know those blue eyes threatened a storm.

"Forgive me, Lord Withersby, but that is exactly what my wife just said."

"Well… But… What I mean to say is… She's a siren." Withersby's face reddened. "Clearly, Your Highness, she has you under her thrall." The man cleared his throat, looking around the room for support.

He found none.

"Oh, she absolutely has me under her thrall," Eric said, pulling his wife into a loose embrace. "Because of the brilliant things that come out of her mouth."

Ariel's lips parted as his hold on her tightened. She let out a quiet gasp as he sat down on his throne and pulled her onto his lap.

The council stared, scandalized, dumbfounded.

Eric wrapped an arm around her waist, settling her against him, his fingers tracing absentminded patterns over the silk at her hip. "Now do as she said. And do not interrupt her again."

CHAPTER EIGHTEEN

The corridors of the palace were long and winding, their gold-trimmed walls and flickering candlelight casting shifting shadows as Ursula padded toward her chambers. The salt breeze crept in from the open terrace doors, filling the air. But beneath it, beneath all of it was the lingering stench of court politics—power, greed, and pretense, woven into the very foundation of this place.

She was bone-weary, her muscles aching from sitting too stiffly for too long, smiling too much, speaking too little. It had been a day of too many glances slid her way, too many suspicious whispers, too many smiles that held nothing but knives hidden behind teeth. The men didn't want to listen to her, the women didn't trust her, and the ones who did look upon her with openness were still calculating, scheming on how best to use her presence to their advantage.

Land courts, sea courts—it was all the same game. She had spent years clawing her way back to a seat at the table, only to find herself exhausted by sitting at the helm of the very thing she had fought to reclaim.

She should have relished this afternoon. The maneuvering, the mental cataloging of allies and enemies alike, the art of knowing exactly who would backstab whom and when.

She was better than them. Sharper. More ruthless. Today, for the first time, she questioned why she wanted back in at all.

The answer to that question should have been easy. She deserved it: the seat, the scepter, the crown, the trident. It had been stolen from her. Triton had taken everything, and she would not rest until she took it back.

And yet, as she reached her chambers, none of that mattered. Not now. Not when the only thing she wanted in this moment was to stretch her fin and curl up in her husband's arms.

Her husband.

She hadn't expected to feel anything about the word.

Hadn't expected her heart to clench in her chest the way it did when she thought of Eric waiting for her, warm and welcoming, with hands that sought her out instinctively, lips that pressed against her skin like he was afraid she might disappear if he let go.

Soon, emissaries would arrive from Triton. They would expose her.

Soon, Eric would learn that it wasn't Ariel who had saved him but the sea witch.

Soon the sea would whisper its secrets—that Ariel had unleashed her siren's wrath upon Prince Phillip's castle, that Eric's most trusted ally had nearly drowned in a wave so massive it shattered stone.

Soon Eric would realize that his fleet had been plagued by pirates, not by coincidence but because of her.

And when that moment came—when everything unraveled and he saw the full scope of her deception—

She would have only one card left to play.

Her song.

Her voice could erase the fury from his eyes. It could soften his clenched jaw. It could wash away the betrayal that was sure to come.

She could make him forget. Could make him forgive. Could make him love her still.

That was tomorrow's battle. Tonight, she just

wanted one more moment of peace. One more night of pleasure. One more taste of the happiness she had no right to claim.

The scent of sea salt and warm water filled the chamber before Ursula even stepped inside. The door creaked open, and she stilled in the entryway at the sight of Eric standing beside a large bath basin. His sleeves were rolled up. He was pouring coarse grains of sea salt into the steaming water. He looked up, caught sight of her, and smiled.

Not the polite smile of a king. Not the regal one he wore in court. It was the smile he gave only to her.

"What are you doing?"

Eric dusted his hands off and nodded toward the basin. "I assumed you'd want to stretch your fin. With everything going on, with tensions uncertain between your father and Phillip, with rumors of attacks—" He hesitated, his jaw clenching before he forced it to relax. "I thought it best if you didn't go out too far into the sea for now. So…" He gestured toward the bath. "I brought the waters to you."

Ursula stared at him, unable to process what she was feeling.

"I was also thinking that I should have a pool built for you here on the castle grounds. We can have sea water pumped in daily, so you never have to be too far from the sea."

He was giving her the sea. She tried to summon a smirk, something teasing, something to brush away the unexpected warmth in her throat. "You're trying to keep me from leaving."

"I'm trying to keep you safe. I want you to have everything you need. But I'm not trying to hold you hostage, siren." He reached for her, tucking a strand of her red hair behind her ear, his fingers lingering along her jaw. "This is your home now. I want it to feel like it."

This man. The people, the palace, the crown, the war—damn it all. She only wanted him. She would lie, cheat, and steal to keep him. And if the world tried to take him from her—she would drown it.

Ursula stepped back. Her hands went to the lacings of her gown. She undid them with a slow, deliberate pull.

Eric's hands tensed at his sides, as if resisting the urge to reach for her. The silk slipped from her shoulders and pooled at her feet, leaving her bare under the dim candlelight. His gaze dragged over her, darkening with heat, with the same raw, unguarded need she had seen in his eyes the night before.

She stepped into the water, sighing as the warmth enveloped her nudity. The salinity was perfectly balanced. Her legs tingled, prickling with energy, with magic, and then—with a shift, a ripple, a shimmer of scales—her fin unfurled beneath her.

Ursula stretched, arching into the pleasure of being back in her natural state, letting herself float for a moment, weightless, free. Then she reached a hand toward her husband.

"Join me."

CHAPTER NINETEEN

Eric stood at the edge of the basin. He watched in rapt fascination as his wife—his siren—slipped beneath the surface. She was bare save for the sapphire gem resting between her breasts. The candlelight flickered against the water, casting shifting, golden ripples over her shoulders, the slope of her back, the long lines of her legs. In the space of a single heartbeat, those legs were gone. Her skin shimmered, her magic rippling outward like a pulse, her thighs fusing, lengthening into something exquisite.

Her tail emerged, iridescent and gleaming beneath the water, deep violet and edged in silver. Her scales caught the candlelight like stardust. The delicate ridges along her fin flared, stretching as if breathing for the first time.

Gods, she was beautiful.

He swallowed hard, the sharp ache of longing punching through his chest. His fingers itched to touch, to trace every shimmering scale, to learn her in this form as intimately as he had in the other.

She turned then, her eyes catching his. Her lips curled at the edges, a teasing, smug smirk. His siren knew exactly what she was doing to him.

Eric had spent the day tending to his kingdom, seeing to his people, listening to their demands, easing their burdens. It had been his duty since the moment he had been old enough to understand what it meant to rule. Since before his mother had passed and his father had abandoned the crown to his vices. For years, his mind had been focused on the crown, day and night. Today, Eric's thoughts had been elsewhere.

They'd been on her. On tending to his wife. On seeing to her needs. Those thoughts had quickly become his greatest joy, his reason for being.

Of course, he had prepared her this saltwater bath. Of course, he had ensured the temperature was perfect, measuring the salinity with painstaking care. Of course, he had arranged for the raw fish and seaweed she preferred, despite the strange looks from the palace kitchen staff. And of course, when she lifted a delicate, webbed hand from the water, her fingers beckoning, her voice a velvet whisper—"Join me"—he obeyed immediately.

His clothes hit the floor in a careless heap as he stepped forward. The heat of the bath licked up his skin as he slid in behind her. He wrapped the whole of himself around her, mimicking how she had wrapped him around her pinky finger.

His siren let out a small, satisfied sigh, leaning back against his chest. Her spine aligned with his as she gave him her upper body weight. Her scales brushed his thighs where her tail curled against his erection. The sensation was unlike anything he'd ever felt—like water running over polished stone, smooth in one direction, catching slightly in the other. It was a delicate rasp, like the whisper of sand beneath the tide or the fine edge of a pearl-grit blade. Some places were soft and silken, others subtly ridged.

He loved the sensation—loved the contradiction of it. She was velvet wrapped in armor, danger cloaked in allure. Her scales clung and shifted with her smallest movements, sending tiny, electric thrills across his skin. And gods help him, but he wanted to feel every inch of her.

He pressed a kiss to the curve of her shoulder, trailing his lips along the damp skin of her throat. Though she'd been in interior rooms filled with cloying perfumes, she smelled of the sea—salt and warmth, brine and something sweet.

He reached for the bowl of crushed sea salts resting at the basin's edge and dipped his fingers in, rubbing the rough grains between his palms. Then he began to work them into her back, massaging slow, deliberate circles over taut muscle, over the knots in her shoulders, down the elegant line of her spine. His siren melted beneath his touch, her head lolling to the side, a soft sound escaping her lips—half sigh, half purr.

"More?" he asked against her ear.

Her response was a slow, languid stretch, her tail curling around his legs beneath the water, the fin brushing over his calf.

Eric was tired, exhausted from the day's responsibilities, but caring for her, tending to her, touching her, loving her—it energized him, made him feel more alive than he ever had before. He reached for the small pitcher beside the bath and poured warm saltwater over her hair, running his fingers through the heavy, silken strands, untangling them with gentle strokes. Her breathing slowed, deep and even, utterly relaxed.

He kissed the back of her neck again. "You're falling asleep on me."

"No, I'm treasuring every second I have with you."

The warm water lapped gently around them. Eric ran his fingers through her thick red hair, rubbing crushed sea salts into her scalp, massaging the tension from her body. Every time she exhaled, he felt the slight ripple of magic in the water.

"I'm keeping secrets from you."

Eric's hands stilled at her words. His heart kicked up, not in fear, but in anticipation. He had suspected as much. He wasn't a fool—his wife was a strategist, a woman who played the long game, who thought ten steps ahead. It was one of the things that fascinated him about her.

He rinsed the salt from her hair, watching the suds swirl into the water before answering. "Are these secrets from the Sea Kingdom?"

She nodded, her fin shifting under the water.

Eric smoothed his hands over her shoulders, trailing down her arms, feeling the tension coiled beneath her skin. "Do they pose a threat to me or my people?"

"I would never do anything to hurt you. Though I'm sure my secrets won't endear your people to me. I didn't factor them in. Only you." She sighed and leaned back against him, fluttering her tail up and fanning her fin out. "I'm good at tactics. At moving people into position to achieve my aims. I see the world as a battle-field. But you… You got past my defenses."

Eric pulled her tighter against him, pressing his lips against the damp curve of her shoulder. "That's good. Because I have no intention of retreating from you."

She huffed a small laugh, but it lacked any sharpness. It was real.

"Do you need my help, siren? Is there something I can do?"

She shook her head.

"Will these secrets cause you harm?"

"No. But… you might be upset with me at first when they come into the light."

Eric tilted her chin up, forcing her to look at him. "Couples fight," he said with an easy grin. "We're bound to have a few disagreements here and there. Likely when I'm too pigheaded to see that you're right and I'm wrong."

That surprised a genuine laugh from her—a delighted sound that sent warmth rushing through him. Eric took full advantage. His mouth claimed hers, swallowing the laughter, replacing it with something sensuous and unguarded. Her lips parted, and he deepened the kiss, tasting the salt of the sea on her tongue, feeling the way her fingers curled into his chest, clutching him like he was her anchor.

When he broke away, their breath mingling, he ran his thumb along her kiss-swollen lips, memorizing the sight of her like this—relaxed, flushed, his.

"I gave you my vow. There's nothing you can say or do, no secret that will make me take those words back."

CHAPTER TWENTY

The tea was bitter. Why humans preferred to drink water seasoned with grass was beyond her. Ursula had been raised to stand on ceremony with foreign dignitaries. Now that she was queen, she set the cup down and didn't pick it up again. It wasn't the drink itself that bothered her—she'd swallowed far worse things in her life—but rather the company that soured the experience.

The ladies of the court sat in their lace-trimmed gowns. Their pearled fingers rested delicately on porcelain cups. Their false smiles arrowed sharper than fishhooks. They were circling her like sharks, their whispers darting just beneath the surface of polite conversation.

"How exotic it must be," one of them—Lady Helena,

Ursula thought her name was—said with a demure little smile, her voice laced with carefully placed venom. "Coming onto land after spending your whole life under the sea. It must be so disorienting."

"Oh, quite," another agreed. Ursula had no idea of the barnacle's name. "I can't imagine how difficult it must be to adapt. Why, walking alone must be exhausting after all that swimming."

"You're quite right," Ursula agreed. "The human body is so… delicate. The wrong touch, and a bone snaps. The wrong step, and you're sprawled on the ground, limbs akimbo. I've always liked that word, akimbo. The sea, you see, does not coddle weakness."

The air thinned, the tension shifting like an undercurrent.

Lady Helena straightened her spine, plastering on a faux smile. "How fortunate, then, that you've married our prince. He's so… generous to take in someone from such a different background."

"Eric is no longer a prince." Ursula's lips curled. "He's your king, and I am his queen. But you are right; he does so love taking care of me, in all manners."

She let her words hang there, let them think of exactly what that meant. A flicker of discomfort passed through the gathered women. Some shifted in their seats. Others cast quick, unreadable glances at one another.

Good. They needed to get it in their heads that they weren't dealing with a pawn or a prawn. Ursula been raised as royalty in dangerous waters, and her teeth were far sharper than any shark's.

She tapped her fingers against the settee, trying to determine the best way to get out of this luncheon. The ladies continued their idle chatter. Their gossip-laced voices washed over her like the ebb and flow of the tide. She hadn't been listening—not really—until she heard it.

"Such a dreadful inconvenience," Lady Helena was saying, tapping a jeweled finger against the rim of her teacup. "The merchants are already in an uproar over taxation, and now with this delay of the ocean liner full of grain, the commoners are getting restless."

The ocean liner. Ursula had nearly forgotten about it. And she'd been right. The ship was now filled with useless grain. If barrels of grain sank to the bottom of the sea, it would do nothing for the seafolk. But Flotsam and Jetsam with their pea brains would only see opportunity and not think it through. Not without her.

Eric needed that shipment. If it didn't reach the docks, his kingdom could be thrown into further discontent, unrest, weakness. Hungry people did stupid things. She would simply have to make sure that the humans were fed and the sea cretins kept their scales to themselves. She huffed, realizing she had more plotting to do.

No, actually she didn't. She could go to Eric. She could tell her husband to send a cutter out to intercept the liner and divert its route away from where she knew the eels would be lurking. The craziest part of the plan… Ursula believed Eric would listen to her.

The heavy doors swung open, and Grimsby stepped inside, his expression grave. "The delegation from your father has finally arrived, Your Majesty. They are waiting in the grand hall."

"The… delegation?" Ursula echoed, keeping her voice light, careful. "From my father, you say?"

"Yes," Grimsby said, looking weary. "Your father's emissary, Sebastian, is eager to see you."

Of course, he would be here. Her father's ever-loyal lapcrab, the one who had watched over Ariel since the day she was born. Sebastian would take one look at Ursula, and he would know.

"How wonderful," she said smoothly, though her nails dug into the fabric of her dress. "I'll be along shortly—I just need a moment to prepare."

She turned before Grimsby could argue, gliding out of the room, pulse thrumming in her throat. She had to think.

She could face Sebastian as herself. She was queen now. But she was Queen of the Coast, not of the sea.

She could make a dash for it. Head back to the docks. And what? Slink back to Flotsam and Jetsam? No, she was not going back to that tide.

Not when Eric was building her an indoor pool filled with sea water.

Not when Eric would be waiting for her each night with salt in hand to rub her tired legs and delight when they turned into a fin.

Not when Eric took her hand whenever he was near her and did the sexiest thing any male had ever done for her by giving her his ear. And listening to her.

Ursula had to admit it; the man was a prize. One that she had earned. One that she would not be giving up.

She was near the back entrance of the castle, where servants came and went. Ursula turned on her heel, ready to ascend the stairs to her husband. She would tell him the truth. He wouldn't turn her away. He'd said he wouldn't when she'd semi-confessed. He might be angry, but he'd promised he would stand by her. There was a silly part of her—a big, shining, silly part—that believed him.

As she stepped a toe onto the first stair, a door behind her opened. A hand shot out and grabbed her wrist. Ursula turned, preparing to give the audacious servant a tongue lashing.

The words caught in her throat. Her eyes went

wide. Her mouth went slack. Because she was looking at herself in the mirror.

"Ariel?"

The girl looked nothing like the pampered sea princess she'd once mocked. Her red hair was a knotted mess, wild as seaweed in a storm. Her gown was torn, streaked with mud and soot. There was a desperation in her that Ursula had never seen.

"What—" Ursula began.

Ariel clapped a trembling hand over her mouth. She shook her head violently and pointed.

Ursula followed the gesture to a heap in the far corner of the closet. A body. A woman. Blond hair matted with blood. Pale limbs curled protectively. There was a rough bandage tied around her head, soaked dark over her ear.

Aurora.

Ursula stepped into the closet. Ariel shut the door and began waving her hands in the sign language she spoke out of the sea. *They're hunting us. The Forest Folk. Maleficent's guard. We tried to kill her. And Phillip.*

This bit had not been in Grimsby's report.

I couldn't marry Eric, Ariel said with her hands. One of those hands found Aurora's, lacing their fingers together tightly. *We love each other.*

Ursula decided the best course for the moment was

to play dumb. "The two of you? I thought you were just friends. You should go to your father and—"

He'd chain me to a rock in the Mariana Trench before he let me shame the kingdom, her niece signed.

Ursula crossed her arms. "So what do you want from me?"

Ariel squared her shoulders, that old royal fire rekindling. *Money. Safe passage. We need to get to the Frost Kingdom.*

"And if I say no?" Ursula asked coolly.

Then I'll tell Eric who you really are, since you're pretending to be me.

Ursula stared at her niece, a slow smile tugging at the edge of her lips. "Look at you. You've grown teeth."

Ariel's chin lifted. She did not let go of Aurora's hand. In fact, she took a step in front of the girl, shielding the bloody princess from Ursula.

As if Ursula had a care about the bloody beauty. The two of them had just delivered the answer to her problems on a silver platter. Ursula reached for the necklace where it rested against her collarbone—the sea-glass and sapphire chain she'd stolen from Ariel's own bedroom the night she'd taken her place. She held it up between two fingers. It shimmered in the dark, a siren's ransom.

"This will buy you safe passage and ten years of soft pillows. But if you take it, you vanish. Forever. You and your sleeping beauty both. You never write. Never sing. Never show your faces again. You are ghosts."

Ariel snatched the necklace, her fingers squeezing it possessively as she stuffed it into a hidden fold of her cloak. Ursula watched the necklace disappear and felt relief. She gave her spoiled niece and her lover her back as she slipped from the closet and shut the door behind her.

She didn't worry about the two being discovered as they fled. Not when they prized their freedom and their love so much. Just a couple of days ago, Ursula would have scoffed at them. But that was before she'd pressed her lips to her own sleeping beauty.

Now she didn't have to tell Eric she'd lied to him. She could just go on being Ariel. She could send Sebastian away without receiving him and never speak to her brother.

She could say goodbye to the Sea Kingdom. She liked the Coastal castle better. It had her favorite treasure just upstairs.

Ursula still might take the Sea Kingdom one day. If she left Triton to his own inept devices, it would continue to decline. If she simply kept whispering in her husband's ear—no.

She didn't need to whisper to Eric. He would listen to her. He would ask her opinion. He would talk it out with her.

The sudden urge to see him, to hear his voice, to taste his lips, overwhelmed her. Ursula made her way up the stairs, up to his office. She didn't bother knocking. She was his queen. More importantly, she was his wife.

She pushed inside, breathless. Eric stood near his desk, speaking with a man. Her husband's face lit up the moment he saw her, as if nothing else mattered.

"Ariel," he greeted warmly. "I'd like you to meet my friend—"

A man dressed in steel and leather, a sword at his hip, turned with a friendly smile. The moment his gaze rested upon her, the man's expression turned lethal. Before Eric could finish his introduction, the man's hand went straight to the hilt of his sword. The tip of the blade pointed directly at Ursula's neck, where her necklace had rested just moments ago.

CHAPTER TWENTY-ONE

Eric leaned forward, elbows braced against the heavy mahogany desk, fingers steepled as he regarded the man across from him. "I owe you for the work you've done along the borders. The trolls won't be encroaching again anytime soon."

Prince Phillip inclined his head. "And I owe you for the troops and supplies you sent. If not for your ships, we wouldn't have lasted through the first siege."

Phillip had always been Eric's closest equal—same age, same crown-shaped burden pressing against his spine. But where Eric had been forged in the fires of diplomacy and endless councils, Phillip had been honed by steel and bloodshed. There was a sharpness to him now—a lean, hardened edge beneath the noble polish.

His broad shoulders bore the memory of armor, his hands the faint calluses of a blade too often drawn.

And yet, despite the scars of war—despite the faint tension that lived in his jaw and the dark bruises of exhaustion beneath his eyes—there was a softness there too. Not weakness. No, it was something else.

Love.

Eric recognized it the way sailors recognized the tide: instinctively, without question. It was in the barely there smile that ghosted his lips when he spoke of his bride. A bride who was not the one chosen for him. That same smile lived in Eric's own chest now, stubborn and undeniable. He'd only ever seen Phillip bloodied or brash. But now… now there was something gentler threading through the prince's war-forged armor.

They had grown up side by side as future kings. Now they sat, both in love with women they weren't supposed to choose. Maybe that was what made rulers into men worth following—not just the battles they won, but the ones they chose to fight for love.

Phillip sighed, rolling his shoulders as if the weight of the past weeks still clung to them. "I only wish I were here under better circumstances."

Eric leaned back in his chair, fingers tightening against the wood. He had a good idea of what Phillip had come for. The signs of battle still clung to him—his clothes, though fine, were worn at the edges, his sword strapped to his side as if he hadn't dared part with it for even a moment.

"You need more aid," Eric surmised.

Phillip exhaled sharply, nodding. "We barely had time to regroup after the trolls before we were blindsided again. But this time, it wasn't monsters in the woods. It was the sea."

"What I don't understand is why would Ursula attack your people?"

Phillip frowned. "Ursula? The sea witch? It wasn't her."

Eric felt something in his chest loosen slightly. He'd seen Ariel's expression when her aunt was accused. He would be happy to deliver this news of the sea witch's innocence to his wife.

The relief was short-lived. Eric opened his mouth to ask an explanation of his ally. But before he could speak, the door to his office swung open.

He lit up at the sight of his wife. She was radiant in silk, her red hair piled atop her head, her sea-colored eyes meeting his with warmth. The weight of the day, the troubles of the court, the chaos of war—all of it melted away the moment he saw her.

"Ariel, I'd like you to meet my friend—"

A sharp sound rang out. The unmistakable rasp of steel being drawn from its sheath. Phillip's sword flashed in the sunlight. And he pointed it straight at Ariel.

Eric was on his feet instantly, but before he could even demand an explanation, Phillip's expression shifted. His grip on the sword loosened. His brows furrowed in deep confusion as he lowered the weapon.

"You are not Ariel."

Eric didn't think. Instinct roared through his blood, hot and undeniable. In a heartbeat, he was on his feet. He yanked his wife behind him, putting his body between her and the man who had been his friend for as long as he could remember. His sword was at his hip, but his hands clenched into fists, ready to tear through flesh if Phillip so much as twitched toward his wife.

"Explain yourself," Eric demanded, his voice low and dangerous.

"Ariel used her siren song to attack me. She called the sea to destroy my kingdom. My castle lies in ruin. My people—my soldiers—dragged into the depths by her call. If we hadn't sealed the gates when we did, I wouldn't be standing here right now."

"Ariel has been with me for days."

"I've already told you, this isn't Ariel. This is not the woman who attacked me."

What madness was this? It had to be the ravages of war that was turning the prince's brain addled. But why wasn't Ariel denying him?

Shock. That had to be it. She'd just had a blade raised to her throat in a place she'd thought safe. She'd come to him, thinking she was safe. And here, in his inner sanctum, she had nearly been assaulted.

Eric wanted to kiss the color back into her cheeks. He wanted to coax a sound from her throat by licking the column of her neck. But now wasn't the time for that. He needed answers from his ally before he made the man an enemy.

Phillip had lowered his sword, but Eric sensed the threat was still in the room with them. Phillip was wrong about Ariel, wrong about her aunt. Grief and anger had clouded his judgment.

Eric needed to reason this out. "Why would a sea princess attack your kingdom?"

"Because Ariel and Aurora are lovers," Phillip responded.

That caught Eric up short and silenced him. He noticed that his siren still hadn't said a word. She wasn't denying any of this. He had been around her long enough to know that she always had something to say. That sharp wit, that unfiltered tongue—it was one of the first things that had made him fall for her.

Yet now she was silent.

And it wasn't just silence—it was the look on her face.

She wasn't shocked. She wasn't indignant. She wasn't even surprised.

A frenzied cry rang through the chamber, full of disbelief and fury. The sound hit like a thunderclap, loud and damning. Sebastian stood in the doorway, his claws curled into tight fists, his bulbous eyes wild with horror as they locked on to the woman at Eric's back.

The crab took a shaking step forward, his voice rising. "Sea witch!"

CHAPTER TWENTY-TWO

Ursula could hear the faint lapping of the tide beyond the castle walls, the distant caw of gulls circling over the cliffs. But inside the office chamber, nothing stirred—not a breath, not a whisper. Every pair of eyes—the crab's, the Forest King's, the Coastal chamberlain's—was on the man standing before her, the man who had vowed his life to hers only one day ago.

Eric did not speak. He turned slowly, his grip on her hand slackening. His face was unreadable. The hesitation in his eyes was enough to make her chest tighten with something dangerously close to fear.

Ursula tore her fingers from his grasp. This had been inevitable, hadn't it? Every man in her life let her down. Why should he be any different?

Squaring her shoulders, Ursula lifted her chin, letting her voice ring out with unwavering authority. "I am Queen Ursula. Wife of King Eric. A princess of seas and sovereign of this coastal land by right of marriage."

Sebastian's bulbous eyes filled with outrage as he shuffled forward. "Queen? Ha! More like imposter! Liar! You tricked the prince into marriage, and now you seek to claim the throne!"

"I tricked no one. King Eric spoke his vows to me. Not to a name. Not to an illusion. To me."

The weight of her own words settled over the room. They were true. Eric had not married her because he believed she was Ariel—at least not in the end. He had chosen her. Over and over again.

He would do well to remember that. He might be prepared to betray her, but he could not break the vows he'd made. She was his queen, even if he no longer wanted her to be his.

Still, his silence was a knife in her gut.

Grimsby, ever the cautious voice of reason, cleared his throat. His lined face was dark with suspicion as he spoke. "How do we know you did not use your siren's song to bend his will?"

Ursula's nails curled into her palms, but she did not waver. Instead, she stepped forward, placing herself fully in the center of the room, under the weight of every skeptical gaze. "A siren's song will not work on her true love."

The words dropped like a stone into the silence. A charged, breathless moment passed. And then, slowly—too slowly—every gaze turned to Eric.

He was standing at the window, staring out at the restless sea. His broad shoulders were rigid, tension rippling through his stance. The man who had placed himself in front of a blade only moments ago, who had kissed her breathless in the bath only last night, who had pulled her into his arms and whispered that nothing could make him take back his vows—he was silent now.

That silly part of her that refused to die demanded that he say something. But Eric remained still, his gaze locked on the waves. A storm was brewing on the horizon.

Ursula had no time for silliness. She had no time for stillness. She had no time for silence.

She turned on her heel, snapping her gaze to Prince Phillip first. "I apologize for my niece's actions. She's a stupid girl, and I've punished her and Princess Aurora with exile from all three of our kingdoms."

"You have no right," Sebastian shouted.

"Do not raise your voice to my wife."

Eric's voice was quiet in the room, but the sound of his command reverberated against every one of the four walls and up to the ceiling. His words, spoken low and even, cracked through the chaos like a thunderclap. It echoed, not off stone and plaster, but down through bone and blood. It was as silent as a great wave, the brief and terrifying calm before it crashed down again.

Sebastian flinched and lowered his claws. He pinched his mouth shut.

Eric might have claimed her as his, but he wasn't reaching for her hand. He wasn't giving her his ear. He also wasn't denouncing her. So maybe… Maybe?

But first, she had another mess to make right. Ursula spun toward Grimsby. "The ocean liner that's behind schedule, we need to send out a gull out to them immediately. Tell them to switch course—there are pirates waiting in the waters for their return."

"And how do you know this?" Grimsby's usual cautious, hawkish expression darkened further with suspicion.

"Do as she says." Eric spoke again, in that quiet thunderclap that crashed over all of them. It was not a request. It was an order laced with the kind of authority that could not be questioned.

Grimsby swallowed his next words, nodded stiffly, and turned on his heel.

Phillip gave one last look at Ursula before wisely following Grimsby out the door. Then the others—the guards, the advisors, the lingering councilmen who had no business being there but wanted to gawk at the spectacle—filed out after them.

The last to leave was Sebastian. The crab gave Ursula a look that said this wasn't over. She knew he would go cawing to the sea king. Ursula would be ready when her brother came to face her.

At last, she and Eric were alone. He stood motionless, his back still to her, facing the window and the vast stretch of sea rolling beneath the sky. The set of his shoulders was stiff, his muscles coiled like a storm battering a ship's mast.

Ursula decided to break the silence. "I told you I was keeping secrets."

"You were keeping *you* from me."

"I lied about my name. But I gave you all of me."

"Because you wanted me to steal you a throne."

"You gave me *your* throne."

He laughed at that. Not the warm, low rumble she'd once felt against her skin like a tide rising to meet her. This laugh was different—sharp, dry, stripped of affection. It cut through the space between them like fishing wire: thin, nearly invisible, but merciless all the same.

For the first time in her life, Ursula felt the ache of regret bloom behind her ribs. She had lied before. Lied to kings, to merchants, to monsters. She'd worn deception like armor. But she had never hated herself for it. And she wouldn't start now.

"You should be thanking me for saving you from her. Ariel is a spoiled, selfish brat. She would have made you miserable."

"My heroine."

She wanted just that. She wanted to be this man's heroine. But once again, she was cast as the villain.

"I'll fix it," she conceded. "I'll take care of it: the liner, my brother, our marriage—"

"No." He finally turned to face her. "I'll take care of it."

His expression was a tsunami roaring toward shore. A surge of emotion, too vast and fast for her to brace against. Hurt crested first, then pain, disappointment, weariness… all of it flashing too quickly across his face for her to parse fully, but each one slicing her open with brutal clarity.

"You can't fix this," she said. "You can't reach the sea pirates, and they are the priority."

"I'll take a cutter and intercept the liner."

"That's not fast enough. I'm faster."

"Don't you dare. Don't you dare go into that sea where your brother can snatch you away from—"

Eric inhaled. Ursula held her breath. She did not fill the silence. She desperately wanted him to finish that sentence.

"You stay here. I'll go and fix the mess you made."

"Your way won't work. You're not listening to me."

"Because you've done enough."

A long silence stretched between them. His silence was the most painful thing she'd ever experienced. But she would not let him see that. She would not let him see the power he held over her.

They stared at one another, the air between them as brittle as dried coral. Her spine was straight, chin lifted with defiance, but her eyes betrayed her—wide and aching, pleading for something she would never ask for aloud.

Eric's jaw tensed, his glare sharp enough to cleave through steel. She tried not to crack beneath it. She wouldn't crack. But her fingers—traitorous, trembling things—quivered at her sides, aching to reach for him.

His eyes flicked down, lingering on the tremble of her hand. For a heartbeat, she thought he would take them. That he would cross the distance between them, thread their fingers together, and pull her close the way he had in the dark of the sea and the quiet of the bath, when words failed and touch was everything.

But he didn't. He looked away. He turned, spine rigid with command and disappointment, and strode out the doors. And for the first time in her life, Ursula was afraid that she'd lost something she couldn't steal back.

CHAPTER TWENTY-THREE

$\mathcal{A}$ hurricane would have been calmer than what was stirring up in the throne room. The storm had no eye—only fury. Nobles rose from their seats like sea-swept trees, voices crashing into each other like thunder against stone. Their silken robes swirled with their gestures, colorful and violent as flapping storm flags. Accusations flew like hailstones, ricocheting off stone pillars and flaring tempers.

Some shouted for war. Others demanded arrest. One even dared to suggest abdication.

Grimsby stood near the foot of the dais. His face was drawn and pale as he clutched his papers like a lifeline, but even he was being pulled into the tide. His usual poise had frayed. Words tumbled out half-formed as he tried to restore order. Beside him, Sebastian's voice rose in a shrill crescendo, his claws clicking in agitation as he decried betrayal and treason and demanded Ursula's head.

The tempest roared, but none of it touched Eric directly. He sat in the eye of it all, focused on the sluggish beat of his heart. He was motionless on the throne, watching as his kingdom tore itself apart before him. Above the gale, he strained for something else—the faint scent of salt and silk, the ghost of a siren's song, the one voice that could calm the storm.

"The sea witch has bewitched you!"

"Triton has played us for fools!"

"This is an act of war!"

Eric didn't move. Didn't react. As the nobles raged on, the weight he had shed just a day ago began to settle back onto him. It pressed against his shoulders. It coiled tightly at the base of his neck. The ache that had disappeared in her arms, beneath her hands, returned, creeping down his spine like fingers of cold iron. The headache he had forgotten now thrummed at his temples, a dull pounding in sync with the raised voices demanding war, annulment, blood. His back, once unburdened, felt rigid, as if the very throne beneath him was turning to stone.

"Now is the time to strike, Your Majesty!"

"You must annul this farce of a marriage!"

"I say we take her head!"

Eric had been resting his head on his knuckles, elbow braced on the carved lion's head of the throne arm. He hadn't moved through the storm of voices, had barely blinked. But now—he straightened.

The motion was slow, deliberate. His spine uncoiled with quiet purpose. His gaze, calm as a still sea and twice as dangerous, swept the chamber and locked on to the one who'd dared speak last.

It was a minor noble from the northern coast—pale, sweating, suddenly aware of how loud his voice had been. The nobleman swallowed hard, his bravado folding like a ship's mast in a gale. He sank back into his seat without another sound, unable to hold the prince's eyes.

Sebastian scuttled onto the dais, his beady eyes alight with fury. "King Triton had nothing to do with this. It was all the sea witch's doing. She's a menace. She tricked you, fooled you."

"Tell me something, Sebastian. How exactly was my wife cast out of your kingdom?"

There were a few throat clearings in the room, accompanied by many more meaningful gazes. Eric knew they were all in acknowledgement of the emphasis he'd put on Ursula's title.

Ursula? The name settled in his mind. She hadn't looked like an Ariel, hadn't felt airy like the name suggested. But Ursula felt right.

"The sea witch was reckless. She put Princess Ariel in danger. Ursula—" Sebastian hesitated, claws clicking together in agitation. "She called the kraken."

The very name of the beast had been whispered for years as the justification for war, for distrust, for every ill-fated ship that never made it home. The Sea Kingdom had wielded the threat of the kraken as a reason for their hostility toward his people, just as his people had used it to justify their fear.

And yet—

Eric's mind reeled back to nights spent tangled in silk sheets and candlelight, when she had let him into her world piece by piece. He recalled her voice, husky and raw. *My aunt saved Princess Ariel's life.*

She'd been talking about herself. She had saved Ariel.

"Some air-breathing fools thought it would be sport to harpoon a mermaid," Sebastian was saying.

A misbehaving child. A harpoon. A siren's desperate call to the only creature powerful enough to stop the slaughter. And for that, Ursula had been cast out of her kingdom?

It couldn't have been the whole story. No, no, it wasn't. She had said no one listened to her. But Eric had. He'd listened to her every word.

He had spent his life locked in this dance of diplomacy, treaties held together with fraying seams, prepared to marry a stranger just to maintain a peace that had never truly existed. All over a single act of desperation. A handful of seamen with cruel intentions. A child's foolishness. Those conditions had brought his siren to him. And now they were what was threatening to tear them apart.

Eric looked out the window. Below, the sea stretched wide and glinting under the midday sun, deceptively calm. And there—moving like a shadow carved from moonlight—was Ursula.

She walked alone, her red hair whipping in the wind, her gown clinging to her like a second skin. She moved past the gates, through the courtyard, and beyond the edge of the castle walls. Toward the cliffs.

She paused at the precipice, the sea churning below her in welcome. Then, as if drawn by instinct, she turned and looked back. Up—straight to him.

He swore she saw him through the distance, through the glass, through the truth and the lies between them. He'd told her not to leave, that he would handle it. But of course she didn't listen to him, just as he hadn't listened to her.

He wanted more than anything to hear her voice in his ear. He wanted to tear through the corridors, down the steps, past the guards and barriers and titles, until he could hold her again.

Ursula lifted her chin—like the queen she was—and

he couldn't help the breathless laugh that escaped him. Even now, she knew how to unmake him with a glance. Even now, his anger melted into longing, frustration folded into awe.

He still wanted her. Would always want her. Even when he wasn't ready to forgive her. Even when she didn't ask for forgiveness.

Then she turned and dove. The wind caught her hair like a banner of defiance. His heart seized—but only for a second.

She was born of the sea. She would hit the saltwater and shed the last of her land-born shape, her scales returning like memory, like power, like truth. She would find her brother. And if that brother did not give her back—

Eric's jaw tightened. Then there would be war.

"I agree with your council," Sebastian was saying, oblivious to the scene outside. "Annulment is the only way. We will find Ariel and—"

"Is the Sea Kingdom in the habit of reneging on its word?" Eric asked. "If so, the treaty means nothing. I held up my end of the bargain. I married the sea princess. You should have ensured it was the correct one."

Eric was done with this argument. Done with his anger toward his wife. He had married the correct bride.

"It would seem the Sea Kingdom is in disarray, and you have far bigger concerns than my marriage. I suggest you return home to your queen."

"King," clarified Sebastian. "King Triton."

Eric shrugged. "I don't know. My wife was pretty determined when she left. Perhaps you should scurry home and check your throne."

The moment the crab was gone, the nobles surged forward again—voices rising like gulls in a squall, all beaks and feathers and noise. Accusations flew like sea spray.

Eric heard none of it. He returned to the open window. He lifted his nose into the air and inhaled.

Salt.

Sea.

Her.

He exhaled slowly. His fists loosened. His shoulders dropped from where they'd been clenched beneath the weight of crown and court.

She was out there. Somewhere in the waves. Not running—not hiding—but fixing what she could, cleaning up a mess she hadn't created alone. She'd told him, more than once, that no one ever listened to her. That men had stolen her brilliance, her strategies, her power, her voice, her song when they replayed her lyrics in their own words.

She'd saved Ariel's life and been banished for it.

She'd saved his life, and he'd interrogated her instead of thanking her.

She had no allies because she trusted no one. Because she'd been taught over and over again that loyalty was a blade you gave others, only for them to bury it in your back. And still—still—she had played the game with him. She had reached across the board, across their pasts, their lies, their titles, and chosen to move beside him.

And what had he done? Left her to face the backlash alone. Just like everyone else had done before him. Just like her father. Her brother. Every smug noble who had silenced her voice and stolen her brilliance.

Ursula had survived banishment. Piracy. Betrayal. She didn't wait for rescue—she rescued. She didn't plead for a place—she claimed it. She didn't beg to be seen—she commanded attention.

The sound of wings broke through Eric's reverie. Feathers beat against the wind as a sleek black gull swept through the window, flapping once before perching neatly on the carved stone sill.

A scroll was fastened to its leg. Eric had sent the gull out over an hour ago to warn the liner. He untied the scroll, eyes scanning the ink as it unfurled. The news he found on the parchment lit a fire under his feet.

Eric turned to face the throne room. He was still

angry—still aching from the betrayal of it all. But more than that, he was done letting her fight alone.

Dozens of expectant faces met his gaze—nobles, captains, advisors. All of them jostling for favor. For power. For position. None of them had the clarity to see the game for what it was. They were all playing checkers on a chessboard. The only way to win was to partner with the strongest piece on the board.

He needed his queen.

CHAPTER TWENTY-FOUR

The wind whipped at her hair, tangling it like seaweed in a storm. Ursula stood at the edge of the cliff, the jagged stone cool beneath her bare feet. Below, the tide crashed against the rocks in frothy bursts, salt spray misting the air and stinging her skin. The sun's rays stretched across the horizon, casting the sea in shades of gold and rose.

She didn't dive. She didn't slip beneath the surface and vanish into the depths where she belonged. The sea called to her, but she waited.

It was a pointless exercise. No one came storming after her. No firm grasp caught her wrist. No voice—fierce and familiar—called her name, begged her to stay. There were no heavy bootfalls pounding the path behind her. No cloak thrown over her shoulders. No arms wrapping around her waist to pull her back into a future she was no longer sure belonged to her.

She had imagined him coming. Had pictured it so clearly; Eric breathless, eyes wild, saying none of it mattered. That she could be Ursula or Ariel or a siren or a liar or all of the above, and still he'd choose her. Still, he'd love her.

But the cliffs remained empty. The only hands touching her now were the wind's, cool and uncaring. The only voice was the sea's, rising and falling like her breath.

Still, she waited a moment longer. Just one more.

She wasn't some weak, wailing thing waiting to be saved. She never had been. She was a queen. And it was time she reclaimed her throne.

A flicker on the horizon. A ship. Her eyes, sharper than any human's, cut through the mist, focusing on the vessel cresting the waves in the distance. The ocean liner was returning. She recognized the curve of its hull, the flutter of its flags, the glint of golden trim catching the light.

It was moving fast. Too fast. Which meant it was in restricted waters; prime tide for pirates, as it was just above the kraken's nest. Seems the captain was gambling twice. Idiot.

That path had been laid with traps, a device rigged by the pirates, meant to summon the beast and sink the ship. It was a calculated ploy, one she had set in motion herself, the final step in ensuring that the kingdom's goods were stolen and funneled into the waiting hands of her treacherous former allies.

She shouldn't care. The kingdom had turned on her. Eric had turned on her. They would brand her a traitor whether she did something or not.

And yet.

Her feet moved before her mind caught up, propelling her toward the edge of the cliff. Damn it all. She had a kingdom to reclaim, a throne to seize. But first—she had a heist to ruin.

Ursula's bare feet whispered over the rocks. She reached the end of the cliff and launched herself into the air, the sea rising up to meet her like a dark lover. The surface broke around her with a quiet roar—then silence. Everything else fell away as the water swallowed her whole.

Her body shifted the moment she hit the depths. Her legs fused, muscles tightening, bones realigning. Silken skin shimmered, split by iridescent scales that rippled from her hips to her toes. Her tail unfurled with a snap of motion, sleek and strong, more weapon than limb.

The transformation burned, but the ache was familiar—welcome, even. She exhaled through her gills, bubbles curling past her shoulders, and then she moved. Faster than a current. Faster than thought.

The cold water kissed her skin, rushing past her in silver sheets. Her hair streamed behind her like red smoke. Her eyes narrowed as the coral reef loomed ahead—jagged teeth in the dark, and somewhere behind them, the massive shadow of the ocean liner, lumbering right toward the trap she'd helped set.

Up ahead, the familiar slither of twin shadows caught her eye. Flotsam and Jetsam moved as they always did, creeping low along the murky places in the water. Their voices slid through the mist like oil on water—laughing, conspiring, hungry.

She didn't slow. Didn't call out. She didn't need to. They would feel her in the water soon enough.

"Ursula," Flotsam hissed, his grin stretching wide, too many teeth behind too little warmth. "Where have you been?"

Jetsam coiled out of a reef crevice beside him, his voice slick as oil. "Word is you seduced the prince. Slipped into the castle like a siren in silk. Tell us, love. How many baubles did you get out of him? A crown? A key to the treasury?"

She said nothing. Because they weren't wrong. That had been the plan once. Sneak into the kingdom. Win the prince. Bleed the Coastal Crown dry and return to the sea draped in stolen silk and power.

But then she thought of Eric standing on the docks, salt in his hair and worry in his eyes. Of his hands cupping her jaw as he'd whispered his vows—rough and trembling, like he meant them. She remembered the way he'd nearly drowned after saving his crewmen. No one had bothered to save him. Except her.

And when she needed him most, he had turned his back on her.

Well, she had been the one to turn her back on him. But he hadn't chased after her.

He'd said he was going to fix the mess she'd made. He probably was. But his way wouldn't work because her initial plan was too good.

Already there were hungry sea creatures gathering in the path of the liner. Sharks and scavengers slunk through the dark, drawn to the sight of a soon-to-be helpless ship. Just like the land folk on the docks, the sea folk in the reef were desperate for scraps.

At least Eric was trying to do something to help his people. Meanwhile, brother dearest and his court kept all the kelp to themselves. The sea folk deserved more than scraps from Triton's tables. But the land-dwellers deserved more as well.

The common sailors, the merchants who worked tirelessly, the fishmongers struggling to make ends meet. Not all humans were villains. Just as not all sea folk were innocent.

And the kraken—it was just another pawn, another beast being manipulated for power, just as she had been.

For too many years, Ursula hadn't played sides. She'd only played for herself. Today she was going to shake all the game pieces up. She was going to do away with the board itself.

"You want to tear that ship apart? Raid what little the humans have? Then what?" she asked, her eyes sweeping the gathering. "The humans will retaliate. The treaty will shatter. The sea will become a war zone."

A rumble of discontent rippled through the predators and scavengers. Jetsam hissed beneath his breath. Flotsam stayed still, his gaze narrowing on her.

Ursula was no longer a pirate. Nor a castoff princess. She was Queen of the Coastlands.

"We do not have to be scavengers. I have the Coastal King's ear. He's a fair man. He listens."

That was the truth. Eric had listened to her. He'd even taken her advice and gave her the credit. He might be angry with her now, but he would listen.

"I have helped you raid. I have lined your pockets with stolen goods. And yet we have always had to keep coming back for more. There's another way. A way where you will no longer have to scrape by. Who's with me?"

CHAPTER TWENTY-FIVE

The wind tasted of brine and anticipation. Eric stood at the edge of the dock, spyglass pressed to one eye, the sun glinting off the brass casing. The salty air stung his throat as he adjusted the focus, his jaw tightening when the image sharpened.

It was just as the gull's note had foretold. The ocean liner—massive, regal—was sailing the wrong way. Through the wrong channel. The waters ahead of it looked deceptively calm, too calm, like a sleeping beast that hadn't yet stirred.

Behind him, boots scraped against planks. "Your Majesty?" came the gravelly voice of Captain Hawthorne, his uniform crisp, his expression drawn taut as a bowstring. "What are your orders?"

Eric didn't answer right away. His thoughts churned

like the sea. That ship had hundreds aboard, cargo, too. The souls and the goods fed trade routes and the livelihoods of countless port towns. But the channel it had taken was narrow and treacherous.

She was out there. He couldn't see her, but he could feel her. Like a current running beneath calm water. Like the hush before the tide turned.

His wife was no fool, no helpless victim of circumstance. She was a tactician. A strategist. Always calculating, always adapting. She saw what others didn't. She moved faster than they could react. Just days ago, she had guided him to the ship flying a false flag—subtly, cleverly, letting him take the lead while she maneuvered the truth into the light. That was how she played: silent, swift, always ten moves ahead.

He knew she was doing it now—somewhere beneath those waves, she was already moving pieces across the board. But what she didn't know—what she needed to know—was that she wasn't playing alone anymore. She had the best player in the kingdom on her side. Him.

They had a chance to stop this—this mess of ancient grudges and sea monsters and blood-slick politics—but only together. That was the key. That was the only way they won. But how could he get to her?

A warship would be a declaration of aggression.

Triton's army would rise. Ursula would be caught in the crossfire.

A cutter was smaller, faster—but fast looked like intent. And to hostile sea creatures, a speeding blade over the water was an invitation to strike.

His gaze shifted down the line of ships. Past the warships. Past the cutters. To the little vessel rocking gently at the end of the dock.

He lowered the spyglass. His hand ached from how tightly he'd gripped it. His eyes never left the horizon. "Hold the line."

The captain blinked. "Sire?"

"I'm going out there myself."

There was a pause. A gust of wind tugged at their cloaks. The scent of kelp and oil clung to the dock like a warning.

"I'll ready the fastest cutter," the captain said at once.

"No," Eric replied, calm but firm. "I'm taking my houseboat."

The boat wasn't fast. It wasn't armored. But no one ever attacked houseboats. They weren't worth it—no treasure, no threat. At worst, sea creatures would surface and bare their teeth to frighten the passengers for sport. But no deaths. No violence. To everyone, the houseboat was just driftwood with curtains. To Eric, it was cover.

The captain turned toward him sharply. His lips

parted, perhaps to argue—but then he looked into the king's eyes. Whatever he saw there had him swallowing his protest. He bowed low.

"As you command, Your Majesty."

A murmur rose behind them. Eric turned just slightly to see a small gathering of nobles—his council. His court. His critics. They stood draped in velvet and fur, gesturing wildly, hurling words like arrows.

"The entire navy should go out and escort the liner!"

"It's madness to send the king alone—"

"He's bewitched! Can't you see—?"

Eric didn't even spare them a reply. Captain Hawthorne ignored them as well. He barked orders with sharp efficiency, dismissing his men.

None of the sailors moved. They all stood at ease but ready. Though ordered to stand down, the navy stayed rooted to the dock, steel-eyed and silent, watching their king prepare the houseboat to face the sea's wrath.

Grimsby, of course, was not far behind.

"My lord," he called, climbing the narrow gangplank onto the boat with more dignity than the moment deserved. "Think about this. You're the king now. You must think like a ruler."

Eric paused mid-motion, one hand on the helm, the other coiling a rope around the cleat. "You're wrong on that front. I need to think like a husband who pissed off his wife."

"Send Queen Ursula a gull and a wreath of sea lilies. That's how your father apologized to your mother."

At least the chamberlain was addressing his wife properly. But it wasn't enough.

"I'm not my father, Grimsby." Eric turned to face him fully. The wind teased the edges of his cloak. His curls were damp with spray. His eyes, though, were steady. "Pick your king. If it's not me, say it now. If it is —get behind me."

Grimsby's lips pressed into a thin line. But he said nothing. Just gave a stiff nod, then stepped aside. "I'm behind you. But I'm not going out to sea with you."

Eric looked to the horizon again. The liner was closer now. Still on the wrong path. Still a breath from disaster.

"I trust her. I trust my queen," Eric repeated, louder now, for any who cared to hear. "She saved my life. We gave each other vows. She won't break them," he said, quieter. "At least… I don't think she will."

And with that, he cast off the lines. The houseboat slipped from the dock, small and unarmored, carried by the tide toward monsters, men, and the woman who could ruin or redeem them all.

CHAPTER TWENTY-SIX

The surface broke like glass around her. Moonlight spilled over the sea in silvery ribbons, catching on the slick backs of creatures that swam in her wake. Tentacles, spines, scales—every beast of the deep that had once answered only to rage now trailed behind her in uneasy calm, their monstrous hunger held at bay not by fear—but by her word.

Ursula floated just beneath the surface, her chest rising with each breath. The salt bit at her tongue. The cool water coiled around her limbs like an old friend, reluctant to let her go. Above, the wind howled low, and the sea whispered higher, a dozen currents brushing against her skin like invisible warnings.

Most of the monsters had relented. They would give her time. Let her arbitrate. Let her speak on their behalf to the man with the crown—if only because she promised something no one else ever had: fairness. A voice.

Eric would give her that much. She was sure of it. He'd listen to her, even if he might not ever hold her hand again.

But not all of the sea monsters had agreed. A few had slithered into the shadows of coral reefs and trench mouths, biding their time. Watching.

Flotsam and Jetsam lingered behind at the back of the party. Their sharp teeth were silent, their long bodies cutting slow, lazy circles at the back of the swarm. Loyal to nothing. Opportunists to their bone-white teeth. But even that was fine. So long as they didn't touch the liner.

Ursula's gaze cut east, where the royal navy waited. Every ship sat quiet at dock, sails furled, hulls gleaming like the bellies of sea serpents. A thousand harpoons ready. None fired. A thousand eyes, watching. Hands at their sides or across their chests, waiting.

But then—there it was. A speck. A silhouette. The houseboat.

Her heart surged before her mind caught up. She didn't need a spyglass to know who was aboard. She felt him—his presence, the pull of him—like a current through her blood.

Eric. He'd come. He was coming for her.

She moved to dive—to swim to him, fast as she could, to throw her arms around the only man who had ever looked at her and seen something worth holding on to—

Pain bloomed white-hot across her side. She gasped. Her body jerked. She couldn't move. She was snared. Not a net. Not a harpoon.

A trident. Barbed. Gold-tipped. It tangled in the currents beneath her.

Her scanned the depths. They came into view. Mermen.

Armored, bristling, gliding like swordfish, their weapons sharpened into pointed declarations. Their spears glinted in the dark like moonlight caught on broken shells. Their formation was tight, rehearsed. And behind them—Triton.

Rising from the deep like a myth turned real, white beard wild in the current, golden crown darkened with tarnish. His eyes found hers—rage and betrayal reflected back at her.

"Of course," she muttered bitterly, baring her teeth. "Of course you'd make an entrance now."

The liner was still crawling toward port, too slow, too heavy to turn.

Eric—her Eric—was out in the open, vulnerable, exposed.

And Triton's army was moving fast enough to wake the kraken.

The water vibrated with the force of movement. Her body ached where the trident had pierced her fin. Still, she twisted, straining toward the houseboat, straining toward him. Toward her king, her husband, her love.

She was being truthful when she'd said a siren's true love wouldn't react to her call. There was no need for them to. On the beach that day, when she'd saved him, she'd sang for him to breathe. His obedience should have been instant. It hadn't been.

Ursula hadn't thought much of it at the time. She'd just assumed the man was closer to death than she could sing him back to life. When he'd coughed up the sea, she'd filled her lungs with air and felt relief. When he'd opened his eyes and looked at her, she'd had to swallow hard at her reaction to him. Because she'd wanted to sing to him.

Not a siren's song. She'd wanted to sing a love song. It was the most absurd sensation, and she'd swum away from it. Away from him. Now she was swimming her fastest to get back to him.

Eric was out there, close enough to see. But not close enough to reach him. Gods, she wasn't sure if she could save herself this time.

Triton rose like a specter from the deep, his golden

trident catching the dim light filtering through the waves. Her brother was out for her blood.

Ursula kicked upward, hard, breaking through the surface. The salty air burned her lungs as she gasped, whipping her head toward the sound of shouting.

Eric stood at the bow of his ship. His body was coiled with tension, his hand on the hilt of his sword.

On the docks, she saw the naval ships and its sailors shift into action. Anchors lifted. Men ran to their battle stations.

Beneath them all, the waters stirred. A ripple. A vibration. It wasn't either army.

The kraken's roar split through the ocean, a sound so deep it rattled Ursula's bones. The sea trembled. Waves churned in a frenzy as the beast shifted from the depths. Its massive tentacles sliced through the water, reaching toward the surface.

She hadn't needed to call it. The sea monster had sensed the war brewing in its waters. Now it would destroy whatever it could find. The nearest thing to it was the ocean liner. From its decks, men armed harpoons that would be useless against the monster and would likely do more damage to the sea creatures who had decided to stand behind her.

Ursula had two choices.

She could sing to the men, twist their minds with

her voice, force them to lower their weapons, to stand down, to trust her.

Or—

She could sing to the kraken, call to the ancient beast and lure it back into the abyss, soothing it, coaxing it into sleep once more, which would serve to give Triton an advantage.

The sea creatures held their breaths.

The sailors braced.

The mermen advanced.

The kraken's eyes locked on to the ship.

Ursula opened her mouth—

And sang.

CHAPTER TWENTY-SEVEN

The houseboat pitched beneath Eric's feet, a toy in the mouth of gods. The sea was chaos—pure, ancient chaos. The ocean liner loomed in the distance, crawling toward port like a wounded beast, and all around it was madness.

Triton's army sliced through the surf, spears drawn, golden armor flashing like lightning beneath the waves. Sea monsters flanked them—creatures out of old sailors' nightmares, their eyes glowing, their teeth bared. And from the deep, he felt it—a pulse, a shift, the roiling stir of something vast and ancient.

The kraken. Its tentacles breached the surface like mountain ridges rising from the sea. In the center of it all, caught between monstrous force and human fear, was his wife.

"Hold fire!" Eric shouted over the wind. But his voice was lost to the storm, to the panic, to the thunder of fins and harpoons.

A harpoon launched into the air from the liner. Eric's heart slammed into his ribs. Another one flew, this one angling—aimed low. Aimed at her.

"Cease fire!" he screamed again, voice raw, fists clenched.

But no one could hear the king's orders from the small houseboat in the middle of the sea.

The houseboat rocked again. Eric stumbled, bracing himself on the slick railing, spyglass slipping from his hand. His throat burned with the taste of bile. He couldn't stop them. He wasn't fast enough. The naval ships behind him were too far. The sea was too deep. And he—he was just one man.

Not a merman. Not a soldier. Not a god. Just a king who couldn't swim fast enough to get to his queen.

He felt the helplessness rise like a wave inside him—thick, choking, the kind that could drown a man before he ever touched the sea. He couldn't save her himself. He had to trust that she could get herself out of this.

It went against every instinct in his body—to protect, to fix, to fight. But he couldn't fight the ocean of waves, a gang of sea monsters, or an army of mermen.

Then his wife—his beautiful, brilliant, battle-tested wife—opened her mouth. And sang.

Her voice rolled out over the waves—not a cry, not a scream, not even a warning. A song. Low and haunting, threaded with power and sorrow and a fury that had been tempered into command. It wrapped around the chaos, wove through the storm. The sea seemed to pause. The wind held its breath.

Seasoned sailors and hard-nosed navy officers stiffened like marionettes caught mid-dance. Harpoons wavered. Eyes glassed over. Fingers loosened on triggers and hilts. Even the creatures of the deep, monstrous and wild, faltered in their charge. The kraken, that ancient titan of shadow and tide, curled back ever so slightly, its massive tentacles swaying in the rhythm of her lullaby.

But not Eric.

He heard her. Every note. Every ache and promise stitched into the melody. And gods, it was beautiful—achingly, heartbreakingly beautiful. The sound of it pierced his soul with memories: of her smile curled against his chest, of her hand twining with his under candlelight, of her body arching against his in the dark.

But it did not drown him.

Because she could not drown him.

His heart had already chosen. She had no power to

compel him, not like this, not with her song. She'd told him the truth; her voice had no sway over a soul mate.

At first, Eric thought her voice was meant for the men on the liner. He thought she'd charm them, sway their hands, ease the fear in their fingers that made them drop their weapons.

But they didn't stop. They aimed. They fired. And she ducked.

The notes of her song didn't rise in desperation, didn't shift into commands meant for men. No—her voice deepened, swelled like the belly of a wave. The tenor of it was meant for something older than the bones of ships. She wasn't singing to the soldiers. She was singing to the kraken.

A massive tentacle had already slammed across the liner's hull, tearing through wood and sending a shower of splinters into the air. The liner listed hard, groaning like a beast, wounded and confused. Before the next strike could land—before the kraken could finish what it started—Ursula's voice pierced the chaos.

The kraken hesitated. Its great eye—black and rimmed in bioluminescent fire—blinked once. Another note rang out, high and trembling. The tentacle withdrew.

Like a beast coaxed back to sleep, it began to sink. Tentacles folded in on themselves as the massive body disappeared into the deep. The sea stirred, a churning belly slowly quieting.

Eric's hand gripped the ship's railing as though it were the only thing anchoring him to the world. She'd done it. She'd saved them.

But the harpoons still flew.

The men on the liner saw her tail, not her crown. They didn't see a queen. Their queen.

Eric was about to jump—screw swimming, screw pride, screw everything—he was going in after her, even if it killed him.

The sea split with a thunderclap of foam and light. Triton rose like a storm given form. Golden armor dripped seaweed and wrath. His trident burned with light, raised high, casting eerie shadows across the deck of the houseboat. Mermen surrounded him in tight formation, eyes glowing with magic, spears poised to strike.

Eric did not back down. He stood tall, chest heaving, sea spray clinging to his cloak and soaking through his shirt. His hand gripped the hilt of the dagger at his belt in readiness.

"We will leave the sea witch to you and your men's disposal." Triton stepped forward, water rolling off him in rivulets. "The treaty stands on the marriage of our kingdoms. I will find my daughter. I'll make this right."

"I don't want your daughter. I want your sister."

"I'll have her fin to you on a platter in moments."

"You touch a scale on my wife's tail and I will gut you."

A flicker of disbelief passed over Triton's face. His grip on the trident shifted. The mermen behind him shifted, uncertainty rippling through their ranks.

"You want…" Triton pointed a webbed thumb over his shoulder toward the battle in the waters. "… her?"

"Get me to her before my men spear her and I'll offer you a concession. No taxes on sea goods sold in our markets for the next two years."

Triton tilted his head as though he was having trouble seeing Eric. "You would offer this," he said carefully, "for her?"

"She's my queen."

"Clearly, you're under her siren's call."

"Or she's my true love and her call won't work on me. Either way, you can make an ally of me or an enemy. But you decide now."

Triton's gaze lingered on him, sharp and weighing. Then he exhaled, the fury in his shoulders softening ever so slightly. He looked at Eric like he'd just swindled him at cards.

Eric was done with this particular game. The King of the Sea wasn't a worthy opponent. The man had lost his daughter, who had brought one kingdom to her knees, and his sister, who had the Coastal King wrapped around her finger. Triton's only use to him was his fin.

"Can you swim fast enough to get me to her?"

The next moment, they were diving. The cold rushed over Eric, the shock of it a spear to the lungs. Eric didn't falter. Didn't fight it. He let Triton pull him under, let the sea swallow him whole.

They moved fast—faster than any ship, faster than any tide.

The kraken was sinking slowly into the waters when they surfaced. The beast was retreating, but his men were not. Harpoons cut through the water, slicing toward the siren, still singing for their survival.

A harpoon grazed her side, a flash of red blooming in the water, a thin ribbon of blood curling through the sea like ink on parchment.

Eric's rage exploded. He slammed himself between Ursula and the incoming barrage. His men faltered when they saw him. The harpoons stopped. But his wife wasn't swimming; she was sinking.

A soft gasp escaped his throat. The water around her was tinged crimson. Her song died on her lips as her body drifted down, down, down—

No.

Eric dove after her. His arms closed around her. Her skin was cool, too cool. Her gills fluttered weakly.

Eric held her close. His heartbeat was a frantic drum

against her stillness. He kicked toward the surface, pulling her up, up, up—

They broke through the waves. Eric gasped for air, but his only focus was her. His arms tightened. His hand pressed against her wound, desperate to stop the bleeding.

"Stay with me," he commanded. He would've sung it. But her eyes closed, and he wasn't sure if she'd heard his song.

CHAPTER TWENTY-EIGHT

*P*ain. A dull, insistent ache at her side. A fire burning low in her throat.

Ursula's body felt heavy, weighted, as though she'd been buried under a ship. Maybe she had. The last thing she remembered was the kraken sinking and the sailors firing harpoons at her.

Maybe she'd sunk them? Would serve them right. She'd been trying to save the fools. It was her last time trying to save men. She was done being a heroine.

She tried to breathe and felt the cool, familiar rush of saltwater flood her gills. Not just any saltwater. This salt tasted of home.

Panic licked up her spine. Had she failed? Had she been dragged back to the depths, shackled, thrown at Triton's feet like a trophy of war?

Her fingers twitched. Something soft and warm twined around them. Not chains. Not bonds of imprisonment. A hand.

She knew this grip. The strength in it, the warmth. Even beneath the water, she could feel his pulse. Steady. Unyielding.

Eric.

Ursula blinked, the murk clearing from her vision. Above the surface, moonlight bled silver over the world. She saw the dark outline of a body, his body, slumped on a hard, unforgiving surface. Not sand. Not stone. A pool.

She wasn't at the bottom of the sea. She was in a saltwater pool. She was inside the castle, in the pool he'd promised to build for her.

She sat up abruptly. The moment she did, Eric's grip on her tightened. His breath hitched. His head snapped up. Then he was on her. Pulling her into his arms, holding her so tightly it stole what little air she had left in her lungs.

Ursula gasped. Eric's grip loosened instantly. He murmured a curse, pressing his forehead to hers.

"I'm sorry. Did I hurt you?"

His hands cupped her face, traced the curve of her jaw, brushed over the damp skin of her throat. His fingers drifted lower to the wound at her side. Pain flared at his touch, but his hands were so careful, so reverent, that she didn't pull away.

"Triton said you needed the sea to heal. So I brought it to you."

Ursula swallowed, throat raw. Her voice was hoarse, rasping, but she had to ask. "Why didn't you give me to him?"

"We can conquer the Sea Kingdom tomorrow, if that is your wish, my siren. But right now, you need to heal."

The water rippled as Eric slid into the pool beside her. His body was warm, solid, grounding. He cradled her close, his arms strong but careful, mindful of the wound at her side.

"Rest," he murmured against her temple. "I've got you. I won't let anything hurt you."

She should argue. Should tell him she didn't need his protection. She didn't need anything from anyone. But the exhaustion tugged at her bones, the ache deep in her muscles too heavy to fight. And so, for once, she did as she was told.

She let herself sink into his hold. Her fingers drifted along his forearm, tracing the lines of muscle, the ridges of scars.

"Are you hurt?" she said.

"Yes, I am. Very hurt. You should have told me the truth."

Which truth was he referring to? She'd told so many lies. But only one to him, and that was a lie of omission.

"You wouldn't have married me if you knew who I was."

"Yes, I would have. If you had told me that you were the woman who saved me from the wreck, the one I fell for before I even opened my eyes… I was out looking for you when I was supposed to be meeting your niece."

Hope fluttered in her chest, unexpected and unwelcome. Still, doubt gnawed at her. "If you knew you were marrying the sea witch instead, would you have hesitated?"

"If I knew I was marrying my true love, I wouldn't have wasted a moment clothing and feeding you." His voice was iron and certainty, cutting through the doubts in her chest like a blade. "I would've dragged you to the temple first."

"You're not angry with me?"

"I'm going to be angry for as long as the bruise on your tail fin lasts. But I'm no longer angry *with you*. Our fight is over." His lips brushed against hers, slow, reverent, full of heat. "Now it's time to make up."

He kissed her. Not like before—not with restraint or hesitation—but like a man who'd nearly lost everything. His mouth claimed hers with aching precision, his hand rising to cradle her cheek, his thumb brushing along her jaw.

"Wait. You're admitting that you were wrong?"

"No, you are very much at fault for this one, siren. You rigged the game. But you also saved the day."

Ursula curled into his heat. "That's something you should know about me. I don't play fair—I play to win. A good queen doesn't wait for the rules to favor her… she maneuvers the board until they do."

"The queen is the most powerful piece on the board, but even she needs her king to clear a few pawns now and then. Speaking of pawns, two eel fellows requested to be employed here at the castle. They said they'd serviced you before."

"Two eels, you say?"

Eric nodded.

"Who serviced me? I have no idea who that could be."

Her husband slid his hand along her waist, fingers curling at her hip.

"I'll always back your play, Ursula. Just promise me one thing."

She would promise this man anything, everything. But she wouldn't tell him that. Not just yet. "What's that?"

"That we stop playing on opposite sides." His voice dropped, more vow than jest. "You and me—same team. Always. Let the rest of the world play catch-up."

"Deal."

He kissed her again. Their mouths moved in rhythm, a dance like the tides. It was apology and promise. Anger and forgiveness. A war they both won and lost in equal measure.

Their lips parted, the taste of salt and something sweeter lingering between them. Ursula held his gaze. She traced a fingertip along his jaw, feeling the roughness of stubble against her touch, the warmth of him soaking into her skin.

"Were you serious?"

Eric's brow lifted in silent question.

"About helping me take back the Sea Kingdom."

He shrugged, utterly at ease, his hands lazily drifting along her back, fingers skimming the ridges of her spine. "If that's what you want. We haven't signed the treaty yet. They don't know where Ariel is—not that I need another bride. One siren is enough for me."

"I don't want the sea crown," she admitted, surprising even herself. "Triton's made a mess of things, and I'm tired of cleaning up after him."

"Then what do you want?"

She took a breath, feeling the weight of her own truth settle in her chest. "I want a say in that treaty."

The corners of Eric's mouth curved upward, his grip tightening around her waist, pulling her into the solid heat of his body. "You can have any say you want," he murmured, brushing a kiss against the damp skin of her temple. "I trust your judgment implicitly."

"Even though I tricked you?"

His grin was slow, deliberate, sending a shiver through her that had nothing to do with the cool night air. He cupped her face, his thumb skimming the curve of her cheek, the edge of her lips.

"You know the saying, my love. Keep your enemies close. Keep your wickedly intelligent siren wife under you."

All the tiredness left her body. She sank to the bottom of the pool and pulled her king on top of her.

EPILOGUE

aveena lay sprawled among the tangled sheets. Her silver hair spilled like frost across the pillow. Her bare shoulders gleamed in the pale moonlight. Beyond the towering window, snow drifted lazily from the heavens, each flake spiraling like a whisper from the gods.

She lifted one hand, palm facing upward, and summoned a single snowflake with a thought. It obeyed. The flake floated toward her, delicate as breath, and came to rest in her palm.

The flake was perfect, so symmetrical, so beautiful. Alone, it was a masterpiece. Joined with a thousand others, it became a force of devastation. A blizzard could bury armies. Starve villages. Snuff out warmth and hope with quiet, merciless certainty.

People should have learned long ago: the cold demanded respect.

Slowly, deliberately, Raveena turned her hand over. The snowflake drifted to the stone floor. At contact with the hardwood floor, it melted into nothing.

Behind her, the bed shifted. She didn't look immediately, choosing instead to trace the last glimmer of the melting droplet with her gaze. Only when the man moved closer did she lift her eyes.

He rose naked from the bed, all golden skin and unguarded laughter, a man who believed—poor fool— that he had conquered the Snow Queen.

He glanced back at her, his smile wide, boyish, painfully trusting.

Raveena tugged the corners of her mouth into a smile in return. A small, brittle thing. A mimicry of warmth she had learned long ago. If he had been wiser, he would have noticed the strain behind it.

"That was amazing, Vee."

Raveena rolled her eyes at the nickname. She let her gaze travel over him, cold and assessing. He was a fine specimen by any standard—broad shoulders, strong arms, a chest dusted lightly with gold. His body spoke of long hours astride a horse, of tournaments won, of idle summers spent in pursuit of glory. His jaw was strong, his spine straight, his stamina impressive in the mindless, bludgeoning way of men raised on blood sport and battlefields. But carnal tactician he was not.

Already she could feel the dull ache blooming between her legs, bruises she would need to tend once he had gone to preen or boast to his men. She would soak them away in a steaming bath, slather herself in oils to ease the sting.

Still. The tumble had been worth it. He was hers now.

Conquered. Captured. Caged.

He moved about the room, gathering the clothing he'd so carelessly scattered in his eagerness to reach her. His tunic snagged on the corner of a chest. One boot kicked halfway beneath a tapestry. At least he was cleaning up after himself.

Raveena exhaled a long, contented sigh at the disappearing mess. That had been the worst part of allowing him to paw at her, fumbling hands grabbing, yanking, scattering as if urgency excused untidiness. While he'd thrust into her, her gaze kept snagging on the his discarded socks even as his rough kisses branded her throat.

Her own gown, of course, had been treated properly. It lay folded neatly across the chaise's arm, safe from unsightly wrinkles, preserving its silken sheen. Even in the throes of seduction, Raveena could not abide disorder.

Chaos might rule the hearts of men, but she was order incarnate. Precision. Control.

And now, surveying the slowly reasserted neatness of her room, the dutiful gathering of garments, she allowed herself a rare moment of satisfaction. The prince might believe he'd conquered her, might swagger home to his father's court flushed with victory —but the truth was as simple, as inevitable, as the snow gathering against her windowpanes.

She had claimed him. And soon, through him, she would claim so much more.

He returned to the bed, leaning into her. She supposed he wanted a kiss. She supposed she still had to play the wanton until their marriage vows were spoken. Then she'd put him in his own bedroom in the western tower and leave him to his hunts while she got down to the business of running her kingdom.

"I'll just make sure the coast is clear before I head out," he said with a wink, pressing a loud, careless kiss to her lips.

Raveena blinked. Then blinked again. "Why would the coast need to be clear? Are you expecting an attack in the queen's quarters?"

"No," he chuckled. "No, attack. But we wouldn't want your stepdaughter to catch wind of..." Here he made a motion between them.

The air around her dropped a degree. "Why would

you care what Snow White thinks?" she asked carefully, testing each word as if it might snap her tongue in half.

He chuckled again. The sound grated. How anyone could think his laugh charming was beyond her. "Come now, Vee-"

"Na." Her voice was a lash of ice. "Rave*ena*."

"Oh. Kay. Raveena. A little fun before Snow and I say our vows is all well and good. But there won't be any vows if she knows I bedded you."

Ice formed on Raveena's breath as she exhaled low and slow. "You still think you're going to marry her?"

He gave a baffled little laugh, as if she were the slow one. "Of course, I'm going to marry her. What did you think? That I was going to marry you?"

There it was. Laid bare. She felt the slow, awful heat rising from her chest to her cheeks—not the warmth of passion, but the scalding brand of humiliation.

He saw it too. Saw the flicker of emotion she hadn't masked fast enough. His smile softened, almost apologetic, the way one might pity a bird that had flown into a window.

"Oh," he sighed. "That is what you thought. Oh, Raveena."

The heat of his sigh was unbearable. For a moment, she thought it might burn her alive. Then she crushed it.

The cold swept in, swift and merciless. She pulled it

around her like a second skin, like the armor she should have never laid down for him. The shame froze inside her, sharp as icicles driving into her ribs, brittle as the frost-crusted edges of a broken heart.

He didn't even see the storm gathering behind her eyes. She didn't care if he saw it or not. He would not be marrying her stepdaughter. That simpering Snow White would not be getting this kingdom that Raveena had rightfully stolen by marrying Snow's father.

Prince Charming was her key to keeping her throne. He was going to take her hand in marriage, not Snow White's. Raveena would have his heart. She'd have it carved out and put it in a box if necessary, but she would have it.

Want to read the Snow Queen's story?
Grab a copy of *Wicked Chill*,
Book Three in the Wicked Evermore series.

ABOUT INES JOHNSON

Lover of fairytales, folklore, and mythology, Ines Johnson spends her days reimagining the stories of old in a modern world. She writes books where damsels cause the distress, princesses wield swords, and moms save the world.

If you liked Ines' Beast then you'll love her Vampires and Dragons. To find out more just visit https://ineswrites.com/ReaderGroup

Want More FANTASY ROMANCE by INES JOHNSON?

Wicked Evermore
Wicked Beauty
Wicked Song
Wicked Chill

The Lunaterra Chronicles

The Beastly Crown
The Beautiful Blade

Immortal Vices and Virtues
Forbid Me
Reveal Me